THE JOB

CARA DEE

The Job
Copyright © 2021 by Cara Dee
All rights reserved

Edited by Silently Correcting Your Grammar, LLC.
Formatted by Eliza Rae Services.

WELCOME TO THE CAMASSIA COVE UNIVERSE

Camassia Cove is a town in northern Washington created to be the home of some exciting love stories. **Each novel taking place here is a standalone**—with the exception of sequels and series within the CC universe—and they vary in genre and pairing. What they all have in common is the town in which they live. Some are friends and family. Others are complete strangers. Some have vastly different backgrounds. Some grew up together. It's a small world, and many characters will cross over and pay a visit or two in several books—Cara's way of giving readers a glimpse into the future of their favorite characters. Oh, who is she kidding; they are characters she's unable of saying good-bye to. But, again, each novel stands on its own, and spoilers will be avoided as much as possible.

If you're interested in keeping up with secondary characters, the town, the timeline, and future novels, check out Camassia Cove's own website at www.camassiacove.com. There you will also see which characters have gotten their own books already, where they appear, which books are in the works, character profiles, and you'll be treated to a taste of the town.

———

Get social with Cara
www.caradeewrites.com
www.camassiacove.com
Facebook: @caradeewrites
Twitter: @caradeewrites
Instagram: @caradeewrites

ONE

How the fuck did we end up here?

I swallowed tightly and peered down into the crib. The little girl was too big for the crib, but it was all we had at the moment. I didn't know what kind of bed a toddler required. I just knew it had to be bigger than the one I'd slept in as a newborn.

"She's cute when she's asleep," Case murmured next to me.

Yeah, she was cute. And terrifying.

I reached down and brushed a finger over her cheek.

"I will murder you if you wake her up," my brother stated.

"It's as if you've forgotten it took us four hours of her screaming to get here."

He had a point. I took a step back and folded my arms over my chest. Well, okay, as scared shitless as I was to shoulder this responsibility, I knew it would be okay as long as we did this together, Case and me. He'd steer us right.

Then Case sneezed, and Paisley woke up with a loud cry.

"Fucking murder me," he whispered in horror.

Casey O'Sullivan

"Ma! Ace!" I tucked my shades into the chest pocket of my shirt and walked farther into the house. "Anybody home?"

Maybe they were at the pool. Mom had gotten lucky, managing to reserve one of the little two-bedroom houses that was like twenty feet away from the community's pool. She'd waited for two years for the area to go from development to finished, and now she could kick back on her patio and still keep an eye on Ace when she was in the water.

I eyed the couch in the living room—or more specifically, the wicker basket next to it where a certain fuckhead stashed his sheets and pillow every morning. That asshole needed to find his own place soon and stop crashing on Ma's couch.

Hearing laughter coming from outside, I crossed the room and opened the blinds. Then I clenched my jaw at the sight of Boone. What the fuck was he doing here? He was supposed to make himself disappear when I picked up Ace. And dropped her off, for that matter.

I slid open the patio door and stepped out, and Mom looked up from her crossword puzzle.

I was surprised she didn't have her laptop here. She was always working on her crime novel.

"You're here! Ace is making friends." She pointed at the pool.

"Hey, Ma." I dipped down and kissed her cheek. "Your hair looks different. I like it."

She didn't demand much from us, but she absolutely loved it when we noticed changes with her. She'd dyed it this week. Fuck-ugly red shade that matched her bathing suit. In a few weeks, it would be another color.

"Thank you." She beamed and fluffed the curls. "And you've met your brother, yes? Boone? Say hello."

I straightened and composed my expression. "Fuckface."

He rolled his eyes and reclined in his seat.

I turned to Mom again. "He's not supposed to be here."

We had a deal, goddammit. No matter how much our bullshit frustrated our mother, we weren't gonna work things out, and she just had to live with that.

"He's been sick, sugar," she explained. "Look how pale he is."

That was his normal fucking complexion. Dark-blond, blue-eyed, overgrown, pale man-child. He had the body of a lifeguard —and not the ripped ones on a sunny beach in California. More like one of those giant trolls who flanked pop stars. A cheeseburger in one hand, a fifty-pound dumbbell in the other.

I hated seeing his fucking face. I wanted to smash him into a bloody pulp, then throw him into the Hoover Dam. All his ugly short-sleeved shirts could follow. Nobody over the age of twelve wore short-sleeved button-downs—or under the age of sixty-five. Except for him. Always. Every day. Open like that, with a beater underneath. *Man*, I hated his guts.

"Maybe if he got off his ass and found a job, he'd feel better." I didn't wait for a response. I wasn't here to fucking chitchat with my idiot brother. Instead, I walked over to the pool and saw my eight-year-old doing laps like a little champion. "Ace!" I recognized her clothes and Barbie towel on one of the loungers, so I picked them up and aimed for the steps.

"Hi, Dad! Is it five already?" She swam closer to the edge.

"Yes, ma'am." I enveloped her in the towel once she got out of the water, and I squeezed her to me until she giggled and wheezed. "Did you pack your things?"

"Yes, ma'am," she mimicked. "Lemme go say bye to Daddy. He's not feeling well. I think he might be pregnant."

"Why? Is he feelin' bloated? Are his tits sore? Is his period late?"

She guffawed and stepped into her dress. "No, silly! But yesterday, he got teary-eyed at a commercial and excused himself. It happened on Tuesday too. Something about pet insurance..."

I frowned to myself as she darted over to Ma's patio, and Ace jumped right up on Boone's lap.

He grunted and winced and nearly flew up from his reclined position, and then he hugged her tightly and peppered her face with kisses.

"I'm gonna miss you," I heard him say once I got closer. "Text me before bed every night, okay?"

She nodded and smooched him back. "Will you come to my game?"

"Have I ever missed one?" he retorted with a wink. "Of course I'll be there."

"Come give Gramma a kiss too, honey," Ma said. "Don't forget your homework on the kitchen counter."

We went through the regular drawn-out Friday goodbye, with Ma fussing, Ace running around to make sure she had everything, and me promising to go through her schoolwork before something was handed in. The kid was brilliant, rarely needed help, but she had an attitude problem with outsiders. If she felt a teacher's question was dumb or too simple, she let them know.

She'd been fluent in Sarcasm before she'd started kindergarten.

Soon enough, we left Mom's house. I had Ace's backpack and duffel in my grasp, and she was the little terror who still found it funny to crawl over the door into my car instead of opening it. The only curse of driving a convertible.

My sweet baby. The car, not my daughter. Back in the good ol' days when Boone and I were best friends, he'd restored my ride for me. A dark-green '94 Ford Mustang convertible, the pride of the '90s, despite what everyone else might say. Everyone was chasing classic cars from the '60s, but not me. My life was a shrine to the '90s, give or take a few years.

I threw Ace's bags in the trunk, then got behind the wheel and pulled out from the curb. Shades on, music on, my girl in a good mood. It was Friday, and everything was right in the world when it was my week with her.

"Hey." I reached into the back seat and grabbed her booster seat. It was the rule. If she wanted to sit in the front with me, she had to grow half a foot and act like a preteen.

She grunted and pushed the booster under herself, then adjusted her belt. Around the same time, I drove out of the gates of Ma's community.

Ace located her neon-yellow Ray-Ban knock-offs in my glove box.

Michael Jackson's "Billie Jean" blaring out of the speakers made me forget why I wanted to know if something had happened to Boone. He wasn't part of my life anymore.

"Do the moves with me!" Ace grinned at me.

Well, I couldn't *not*. If one listened to MJ, one moved to the fucking beat.

We bobbed our heads and lip-synched like pros, complete with turntable gestures, "ow!"s, "ooh!"s, "ahh!"s, and crotch grabs.

Five minutes later, I pulled into the Walmart parking lot, and we'd moved on to "Beat It."

"Beat eeeeet!" Ace sang—or yelled—and nodded rapidly. Her fingers hit the imaginary keyboard too, 'cause she fucking rocked like that. "Beat it, beat it!"

I grinned and killed the engine, but the fun didn't stop there. We moonwalked into the store, shared a chill when we got blasted with the icy AC, and I grabbed one of those baskets on wheels while Ace got a kiddie cart.

"What's on your list?" I had mine somewhere... There. Tucked into the back pocket of my jeans.

"Freeze pops!" she declared.

I nodded. "Definitely getting freeze pops."

She tapped her chin as we started our weekly grocery run. "Pizza?"

"Obviously."

We started in the frozen food section and filled up the basket pretty quickly. Pizza, breakfast burritos, burger patties, sausage patties, taquitos... We said hello to our dear friends Pillsbury, DiGiorno, and Jimmy Dean. Then we continued to bacon and shredded cheese, eggs and milk, and last but not least, waffles, four boxes of Pop-Tarts, bread, and some cookies.

"We forgot salad!" she exclaimed.

I squinted at her and scratched my neck. I needed to trim my beard soon. "Uh..."

She sighed and gave me a *look*. "I'll go get it."

Yeah, she could do that, if she insisted. We had vegetables at home. I wasn't an animal. We had pickles, ketchup, a bag of frozen peas, and sweet corn.

While I waited for her to return, I scanned my list to make

sure we had everything. We were good on condiments, soda, snacks, and coffee. I needed to replace my water filter, but that could wait another couple weeks.

"Daddy, I'm cold."

I turned around to see she'd come back. At the top of her cart was a collection of small ready-made salads and fruit cups.

"Because you're still wearing your bathin' suit underneath the dress." I pushed down the sleeves of my denim shirt and unbuttoned it. "Don't drag it along the ground." It'd taken me hundreds of washes to get it perfect. Soft, faded black, well-worn. I draped it around her shoulders and tied the sleeves around her neck, and she giggled and called it her new cape.

"I can be your super-strong sidekick," I said.

She bit her lip. "*Are* you super strong? Like Dad?"

What the fuck? I'd been working out like mad lately. Even my abs showed! But I wasn't gonna flex in front of my daughter. It was probably weird.

Comparing me to Boone was harsh, though.

"If you can't see my impressive biceps, we need to have your eyes checked," I grumbled.

"I don't think anyone can see past the impressive mustard stain on your tank," she replied frankly.

I peered down at my beater and winced. "I went to Costco for lunch."

"Great, now I want a churro," she huffed. "Can you ease my pain with a new nail polish?"

I laughed. "You fuckin' drama queen. Sure, go pick out a nail polish."

She strutted off with victory written all over her, and I got to stand right there and watch our shit. My daughter had me too wrapped around her finger sometimes. She was too much like me sometimes as well. One might even think we shared genes.

But at the end of the day, she was just like her mother—God rest her wild soul.

My phone rang in my pocket, and I was surprised to see my cousin's number. We hadn't talked in a while.

"Darius, how the fuck are you?" I smiled. We didn't share genes either; he was Boone's biological cousin, but we came from families that picked up strays left and right. I'd once been a stray, just like Ace.

"I'm good, kid. All good," he answered. "How's Vegas?"

"Hot." I eyed a guy walking past. "What can I do for you, cuz?"

"I have a job for you and Boone," he told me. "Willow's gonna send you all the information you need." That would be his tech-savvy little sister. "Pretty straightforward—recon work, virtually no pay."

I grinned. "My favorite kind. How'd you know?"

He chuckled. "When push comes to shove, it's more of a favor, but there will be plenty of opportunities for you and Boone to collect a reward from our target."

Color me intrigued. Darius used to be a private military contractor, but he must've taken a break from retirement if he was calling *me* about a job. Unless he wanted to hire me at his restaurant outside of fucking Seattle, and evidently not. He was also a good guy. He came from a family of good guys. But outside of the occasional family reunion, our paths didn't cross, so to speak. Except for that one time he sent a couple buddies my way for intel.

"You can count me in," I said. I trusted him, and I was always on the lookout for my next job. "Boone's another matter. We haven't been on speaking terms for the past four years."

"Why the fuck not?" Darius demanded. "Shit was good when we saw each other last year."

No—far from it. "We're good at pretending when we have

to, I guess." Boone and I kept our most vicious fights far away from our daughter. She was used to the silent treatment he and I gave each other, and at the most, she'd been around a few bitch fights. But we pulled our shit together for her soccer games, recitals, and our family reunions.

"How does that even work with Ace?" Darius asked. I could practically see his frown through the phone. "You share custody?"

"Essentially." It'd never been the plan for Boone and me to live together in the first place, but since when did life give a flying fuck about anyone's plans? Shortly after Tia died, we found out she'd wanted *us* to raise her girl. Two screw-ups and a toddler—nothing could go wrong. Except, we'd moved in to a small apartment together and showed the world that precisely *everything* could go wrong.

I hated thinking about it. I hated being reminded of it. "I don't wanna get into the details," I said, peering down an aisle to see if Ace was coming back anytime soon. "Long-ass story."

"So we'll save it for another time," Darius said. "But you better patch shit up with him, kid, because I need you both on this. You'll hear from Willow tonight." The fucker hung up on me. Was he even ten years older than me?

"I'm not a kid," I bitched at the phone. Thirty-five years old and called kid... Fuck you, cousin.

Patching things up with Boone was outta the question. It'd be like building a bridge from desert sand.

When Ace returned from the cosmetics aisle, we made our way to the registers and decided to have patty melts for dinner. Whatever information Willow had for me, I'd work out on my own. I wasn't gonna worry about it.

"Is the porch done yet?" Ace asked as we walked out of the store.

"Almost. It just needs a coat of paint." I was mostly glad the hammerin' and drillin' were done.

I'd been stoked to learn that the trailer park where I lived got a new owner last year, just six months after I'd moved in to my run-down single-wide. Repairing and renovating the inside was a responsibility I had no problems handling myself, but the exterior fell on the owner of the park, and the previous one hadn't given a fuck. Then the guy who'd taken over had announced that all trailers would get a paint job, the double-wides would be given a small deck in the back, the single-wides a front porch, and we'd get new mailboxes. Five months of constant construction had followed, waking me up at the ass-crack of dawn.

The park looked a hell of a lot better now. The owner had delivered on his upgrades, without raising the lot rent too much. Less concrete, more grass and trees. The playground wasn't a tetanus hazard anymore, and the community pool had been resurfaced.

Reaching my car, I popped the trunk and stashed the groceries next to Ace's bags.

Ace climbed into the back seat, which was unlike her, but when I passed her, I saw the several reasons tumbling out of my shirt. A bunch of shit just fell out when she opened it. Without a care in the world, she started browsing through her loot. Nail polish, body glitter, nail stickers, some candy, a pack of gum... I blew out a heavy breath and bent down, resting my arms on the edge of the door, and I scratched my eyebrow with my car key.

"Ace. What the fuck have we said about shoplifting?"

She looked up at me, eyes wide with innocence. "No one saw me! I swear. And I made sure there were no security tags."

"I don't fucking care." I clenched my jaw, irritated as fuck, and pinned her with a serious look. "We don't shit where we eat. You're here every goddamn week—either with me or with

Gramma—and if you get caught, you can't come back. You hear me?"

She dropped her gaze and chewed on her bottom lip.

It robbed me of some of my anger, and it became a struggle to stand firm. "I'm not fuckin' around, Paisley." Using her real name meant business. She knew that. "Don't shoplift here again, okay?"

"Okay, I won't," she mumbled. "I'm sorry, Daddy."

Fuck. She looked up with those big puppy-dog eyes of hers, and when they flooded with unshed tears, I didn't stand a motherfucking chance.

"Put your seat belt on," I muttered and got behind the wheel.

Kids.

TWO

"Are you gonna tell me what's wrong?" I asked.

It was the main reason I'd driven us straight out into the desert after we'd dropped Paisley off at Ma's place. We were supposed to work, but Case had been acting weird all week. Strung tight, rattled, lost in his own world.

The desert was his place to refocus. It wasn't the first time I'd pulled into a rest stop near Red Rock, and it wouldn't be the last.

He paced in front of my truck and lit up a smoke.

"I'm starting to like the kid," he blurted out eventually. "It's freaking me out. Today when I picked her up at day care, I told some bitch off for speaking baby talk with her. I hate that

13

shit. But it was the feeling, you know? Someone was crossing a line, and I felt this urge to protect the girl from it."

It was too soon to grin. It would only piss him off. But the relief... Not to mention the warmth that filled my chest. It felt good. I leaned back against the truck and let him get it all out.

"She was supposed to be this annoying kid that Tia was forced to bring along everywhere because she couldn't find a sitter," he said, still pacing. "We were never meant to even like Paisley, Boone."

I knew that. There'd been no slot for a kid in our life. No place where we could sit a kid down and go, "Okay, so she's part of it all now." But things changed.

Everything had changed.

"They're fast," Ace noted.

"Yeah." I stood behind her on the sidelines of the soccer field and ran my fingers through her crazy long waves, waiting for Boone to show up. When our girl wanted a braid, he was much better. I could do a haphazard ponytail at best.

The team they were facing today ran around on one half of the field, close to where we were standing, and I liked Ace's way of preparing. She could warm up anywhere, but she could only study her opponent right here and now.

"You'll be on the lookout for that number nine," I said.

"I was just thinkin'." She nodded. "By the way, do you love me, Daddy?"

I shrugged to myself. "You're all right, I guess."

She giggled and peered up at me.

I smirked and dipped down, pressing a smooch to her forehead. "Of-fucking-course I do. What do you want, and how much is it gonna cost me?"

She knew that one. "Lunch at Denny's."

I furrowed my brow. "We already said we were going after the game."

"Yeah, but..." She turned around to face me, and she grabbed my hand. Then she unleashed the doe eyes on me. "I want Dad to come along."

Fuck.

This was one of those times I didn't allow myself to hesitate or get bitchy. "Okay." I nodded and swallowed the resentment that bubbled up. Not at her, just...our fucked-up situation. I didn't wanna see him more than I had to. "The three of us will go out."

"Yes!" She fist-pumped the air, only making me feel like a dick. "Just one more small thing." She pinched her fingers together to demonstrate how small. "I need you to admit that 'The Sign' is the best song Ace of Base ever made."

Get the fuck out with that nonsense. I laughed at the ridiculousness and folded my arms over my chest. "You've lost your goddamn marbles. It's the most *overrated* song by them."

Everyone in their right mind knew it was the underdog "Life Is a Flower."

Ace couldn't argue with me because I was right—or because Boone showed up and she forgot I existed for a beat. She ran over to him and jumped into his arms, to which he picked her up and positioned her on his hip like back when she'd been little.

To him, she was still tiny, I guessed. He dwarfed most people around him, including me, even though he only had a couple inches on me in height.

Fuck him.

"Can you braid my hair?" she asked, holding up a rubber band.

"Sure thing." He set her back on the ground when they

CARA DEE

reached me, though he paid me no mind whatsoever. Not even a hello.

Asshole.

"You're coming out to lunch with us afterward, just so you know," Ace mentioned to him.

"All right." Boone frowned to himself but made no further comment, and he didn't look my way to confirm or ask anything. He just trapped the rubber band between his teeth and started braiding Ace's hair.

Something was wrong with him, and it pissed me off. He looked tired and couldn't pretend to be happy to be here. He usually loved coming to her games.

As soon as he finished with her hair, Ace beamed up at him and gave him a big hug before she ran off to join the team. Her coach gave her a smile, but the look he sent *me* from halfway across the field was anything but friendly.

I blew him a kiss.

He was just pissy because I'd gotten into a heated argument with the ref once. Or twice. A few times. It happened.

With the game about to start, I bent down and picked up the two camping chairs I'd brought and my cooler and walked off to the side. More parents had shown up in the past ten minutes, and I was already on a tight leash. If I wasn't on my best behavior, they'd suspend me from attending permanently, and it wouldn't surprise me around this bunch of prissy bitches if blocking the view was an infraction.

I glanced over my shoulder and noticed Boone wasn't following. "Oi. You comin' or not?"

He looked my way, visibly exhausted, and made no reaction. He followed, but his face was blank. It was as if someone had punched the life out of him.

It rattled me. It freaked me the fuck out. My hatred toward him took a shitload of energy to maintain, and if something was seriously wrong with him, I feared what it would do to me. I could already feel a rock of worry growing in my gut.

I unfolded the chairs in a spot where we'd have the perfect view of our daughter scoring goals, and I sat down and opened the cooler.

"You want a beer?" I asked.

"Sure."

I popped two cans into a couple koozies and handed him one.

Like shit attracted flies, one of the mothers was quick to come over to us.

"You can't drink beer here," she snapped.

I eyed her over the brim of my shades and held up my can. "Are you blind? It says right here." I pointed to the text on the koozie. "'It's just soda, dumbass.'" Last year's Father's Day gift from Ace, with help from Boone. I'd helped her order a customized tool belt for him. Hot pink, just like my koozies.

"You think this is funny?" The woman did not like me. "For heaven's sake, it's ten in the morning."

That one pissed off Boone. "Never you fuckin' mind what we do at ten in the mornin'. Take a hike."

For one brief second, I was flooded with energy and memories from better times when it'd been Boone and me against the world. When it'd been us, like a team, raising Ace together. Working together. Spending most of our time together.

It was a punch in the gut.

The woman sneered at us before she stalked off and muttered about her love for the O'Sullivan boys.

I interpreted it that way, at least.

I leaned back in my seat and took a swig of my beer, and fuck, it tasted good. Ice-cold beer, sun shinin', about to watch my daughter kick ass on the soccer field. I'd had worse mornings.

"You coulda said hello earlier," I pointed out. "No need to be rude."

Boone let out a breath and faced the field. "Don't start with me, Case. If I say hello, you tell me not to talk to you. If I say nothing, I'm rude. Just gimme a break today."

Funny how quickly that feeling from our glory days disappeared.

The rock in my gut doubled in size as I sat there and side-eyed him and sipped my beer noisily. Back in the day, he would've whacked me upside the head. Now, nothing. Not the slightest reaction.

I shouldn't bother. I hated him, right? He'd hurt me too fucking much. He'd broken the only promise I'd ever asked him to uphold. More than once. The last time, almost four years ago, became too much for me. Even though he didn't know, even though he'd never intended to, he'd shattered my fucking heart.

I'd walked away. I'd told him he was dead to me.

Three beers and two Slim Jims got me through the game. Our team lost, but Ace had delivered two goals, so she still had every reason to be proud of her achievement.

We met up at the nearest Denny's, and Ace and I were seated when Boone stepped out of his truck out in the parking lot. I knew what he liked, so I'd already ordered for him. My stomach snarled with hunger, which almost hurt because of the worry I couldn't let go of.

At some point during the game, I could've sworn Boone's eyes looked glassy. For no apparent reason.

"What took you so long, Daddy?" Ace glared playfully as he sat down next to her.

"Had to stop for gas." He kissed the top of her head. "Y'all ordered?"

I nodded once. "I got you your usual combo."

"Thanks." He rested his arms on the table and cracked his knuckles, drawing my attention to his ink. We were both tatted up all over, and I liked his tribute to Ace. The little aces of spades across his knuckles, and then on the side of his hand, in cursive writing, it read Aisley Paisley, which had eventually morphed into her nickname Ace. Boone still called her his Aisley Paisley sometimes, and Ace pretended she loved it because she loved him. More than that, she was fiercely protective of him.

A feeling I used to relate to a fuckload.

Despite his intimidating stature, Boone was the sensitive bastard in the family.

Ace's teddy bear daddy.

I swallowed the grief that threatened to put another dent in my armor of hatred, and I clenched my jaw and looked away.

I wasn't gonna be able to let this go. Angering him, bugging him, saying things that stung, was nothing. It was even a stupid goal of mine. But this was something else. It wasn't about cuts and scrapes anymore.

His hurt, or whatever it was, ran deep.

Our food arrived, and I nodded in thanks and grabbed my fork. Ace and I usually shared our meals when we were here, one stack of pancakes and one order of toast, scrambled eggs, and sausage. The fact that Boone tucked into his two plates filled with all kinds of food wasn't necessarily reassuring, because he was an emotional eater. The hash browns disappeared in three stabs of his fork, and then he was drowning his pancakes in syrup while he went for his bacon and eggs.

It was time to say something. It was time to forge a connection so I could have some time to figure out what the hell was up with him.

"Darius called me the other day," I said.

Ace's dark-brown eyes lit up with excitement. "Is he visiting? Is Uncle Ryan coming too? Can he bring the babies?"

"Slow down, hon," I chuckled. "I don't know yet. It's for a job." I slid my gaze to Boone and swallowed my dread about what this could do for my mental health. "I told him we'd take it —together."

He frowned and wiped his mouth on a napkin. "What kinda job?"

"Recon, mostly."

There was a big fish named Alfred Lange who needed to be fried. It would be Boone's and my job to lay the groundwork.

Darius had been right. I wouldn't be able to do this on my own. I'd been planning on calling a couple friends who were heavily connected, but it went without saying that I preferred to work with my brother. I couldn't deny that.

"I thought we didn't take jobs together anymore," Boone said.

Yeah, well. I thought I had an estranged brother who didn't cry at insurance commercials and when watching our daughter play soccer.

Shit changed.

It didn't escape my notice that Ace was stuffing food in her face while watching us like a spectator at a tennis match.

"You think too much," I settled for saying. "Come over tonight so we can go through the intel Willow sent me. Ace can have a sleepover with Gramma."

"Yes, I sure fucking can," she replied with a grin.

I winked at her.

THREE

"Pipe the fuck down!" Case yelled and banged on the wall. Our neighbors were at it again. If they weren't screwing too loudly, they were using each other as punching bags.

I sat at our tiny kitchen table and tried to get Paisley to eat more.

But good luck getting her to finish her mac and cheese when Case was yelling up a storm. Her dark eyes widened until they were almost round, and she sat stiff as a stick in her booster seat.

"Don't make me bring a baseball bat over there!" Case shouted.

I cleared my throat pointedly. He was one curse away from scaring the poor girl.

He glanced back at me, then at Paisley, and scratched the side of his head. "Come here, sweet pea. You can help me." He picked her up from the seat and returned to the wall. "Like this." He started banging on the wall again. "Stop including your neighbors in your fights!"

Paisley was no longer scared. A big smile lit up her face, and she began pounding her fists on the wall too. "Stop it, stop it, stop it!" she yelled.

"That's my girl." Case hugged her tightly.

"Oh, Casey. *Why?*"

I smirked. "Why what?"

Ma sighed heavily and shook her head. "You know very well. You shouldn't encourage her like that. The pins are bad enough."

I couldn't help but laugh. "It's a joke. It's funny!"

And the pins were priceless. Ace was mildly obsessed with funny pins that she could fasten on her backpack and clothes.

"Only if people know the whole story," Ma grated.

She piped down when Ace reappeared in the hallway. She'd bolted as soon as I'd stopped the car because she had to pee.

I bent down and gave her my cheek. "Be good. I'll pick you up after school tomorrow."

She nodded and kissed my cheek. "You be good too, Dad. Okay?"

"I promise." I kissed her on the forehead and spotted Boone coming from the kitchen.

He managed a grin at her T-shirt. "I fuckin' love it, baby."

"Right?" she exclaimed. "Dad took me to a place at the

outlet mall yesterday where you can personalize your clothes just like that." She snapped her fingers.

I smiled and scratched my nose.

Mom huffed and threw her hands up in surrender before she just walked off.

Poor woman.

In my opinion, a tee with the words, "Muh daddy's muh uncle, muh uncle's muh daddy" was simply brilliant humor.

From an early age, Ace had loved to slide that into conversation with everyone from the old guy at the gas station to the girl taking our order at Wendy's. One way or another, she let people know her fathers were brothers.

"You ready to go?" I asked Boone.

He inclined his head. "I'll follow you."

Oh, right. He hadn't actually been to my place.

Ten minutes later, with a remix of "Mr. Saxobeat" pouring out of the speakers of my car, I rolled into Paradise Parkview with my brother in tow. I nodded my head to the beat and drove past the main office, the playground, and took a right to get to 4th Lane where I had my trailer. But apparently, we weren't allowed to call them trailers anymore. The new owner was putting "manufactured homes" in all the brochures and sounded like a broken fucking record. Even into the name of the park, which was actually now Paradise Parkview Manufactured Home Club, your affordable sanctuary on the edge between Paradise and Winchester.

Giving the trailers a fresh coat of white paint and renaming the park was like giving a hot dog a French name and calling it fine dining.

I parked next to my trailer and sat there while I waited for the song to end.

It'd been ages since I'd gone out. It was time. I needed to hit up a club soon or something, maybe get laid.

"Are you comin', sunshine?" Boone hollered.

I sighed and killed the music, then stepped out of my car. "Usually not in front of people."

He snorted and averted his gaze, taking in the closest surroundings. He'd parked a little too close to my mailbox. Fucker. "I guess that sucks for your boyfriend."

Huh? "I don't have one, so..." I climbed up my porch, where I wanted to spend many future evenings with Ace, and retrieved my keys. The porch was gonna get painted on Tuesday, after which I could finally put out the grill I'd bought. It was waiting in the carport, along with a table and four chairs. Ace had made plans for us to have game nights.

"If you wanna keep it private, fine, no need to bullshit," he muttered behind me. "I saw you getting pizza together at our place 'bout a year ago—then again a couple months after at a gas station."

What the hell was he— Oh. He must've seen me with Dave. "We went out a few times, that's all." I unlocked the door and went inside to crank up the AC. "Why would I wanna keep that private?"

"Uh, I don't know, maybe because you've never brought anyone home before?" he argued. "There's also that one time you told me not to show my face near you if I was with a woman, and when that happened, you cut me outta your life."

That one time? One fucking time?

Embarrassment and anger burned hotly, and in a split second, I regretted everything that'd led up to him being at my goddamn house right now. This wasn't gonna work.

I threw my keys on the table next to the door and crossed

the living room, went into the kitchen, and grabbed my vodka from the freezer.

"Jesus Christ, this place is tiny." I heard him say.

Feel free to fuck off, asshole.

It wasn't tiny. It was...compact. Ace and I didn't need more. The kitchen was a little crowded when she and I prepared dinner together, and only my daughter would call the bathroom spacious, but the rest was okay. She had her own room in the back, I slept in the living room, and I'd turned the closet space across from the bathroom into my restricted zone. It was where I kept all my work shit, equipment, my safe, all the valuables.

"At least I'm not acting like a child and sleeping on Mom's couch," I called back.

"Okay, trailer trash."

Wait—he'd said something before. It just registered. I poked my head out of the kitchen and frowned. "What the fuck is *our* place, anyway? You said you saw me get pizza with someone at our place."

He waved it off dismissively and stared at the pullout couch I hadn't made this morning. "I didn't mean it like that. Giordano's—we used to get pizza there after a gig."

Oh. I laughed at the fucker, even as nausea crawled up my throat because it brought me back. Boone had always been sweet. Protective, nostalgic, sentimental. He loved traditions and holidays and birthdays. He loved showing others how much he cared. And at one point, I had been at the center of his attention.

It was all his fault that I'd gotten confused at an early age. His fault that I'd always struggled to connect with other guys. His motherfucking fault I'd realized, at the age of twenty, that I was in love with my own brother.

I hadn't told him never to date or be with women; I'd asked him pleadingly, that when we worked together, he didn't bring any women around *me*, because it fucking hurt to watch. It'd killed a part of me every goddamn time I'd seen him flirt with women. Only for him to get back to treating me like I was the best thing since sliced bread as soon as the bitches left the room.

I couldn't go down that road again. My twenties consisted of daily heartbreak, being pulled in, pushed aside, burning jealousy, anger, fantasies, and dejection. And he'd never know.

I poured myself a glass of vodka and took a big gulp.

"Let's just do this job together so we can go back to not speaking to each other again," he said.

"Fine by me." I took another long swig of vodka, emptying my glass, before I left the kitchen. After punching in the four-digit code, I opened the closet and grabbed the laptop I never hooked up to the internet. It was one of four that I used, and any data was transferred through USB sticks or other safe channels. The encrypted file Willow had sent me had gone straight to the one where I never used my own name.

Ace once asked me why I needed so many laptops, and I'd given her a long-ass harangue about privacy and Big Brother watching. Of course, then I'd gotten a call from Ace's school because my girl had gotten on her own soapbox to tell her class-mates that people in general were government-owned sheep.

Kids said the craziest things.

Boone had turned the pullout into a couch by the time I rejoined him. We sat down together, and I booted up the laptop on the coffee table.

"You got anything to drink?" he asked.

"Help yourself." I inserted my password. "Grab me a beer while you're at it."

He rose without a word, and I watched him trail into the kitchen.

If he were me, he'd only get something for himself. I was the catty one when I was pissed or hurt. He became silent and possibly depressed. That's what I had to figure out. And if he was depressed, I had to do something.

I'd pulled up all the documents from Willow's file when Boone returned with beer for both of us.

"All right, so the target is an Alfred Lange and his crime organization," I said. "At the end of October, there's a reservation at the Venetian traced back to Lange, and it includes a party venue and a block of suites. Darius wants us to find out as much as possible about their stay, their plans, their reservations, and, more importantly, about Lange's son who lives here in town. His name is AJ Lange, and he works for the Gaming Commission."

I angled the laptop closer to Boone so he could see the information I had. Which wasn't much—not even the complete hotel reservation, just a date and some minor details.

Lange dealt in coke, diamonds, and human trafficking. He was based outta Florida, was presumed to travel with heavy security, and Willow had no idea just how many shell corporations he sat behind. So far, she'd dug up seven.

Boone and I rarely asked questions when we got gigs like this one, but I couldn't deny that I was curious about our cousin's motives. If this was a contract from whatever PMC he'd worked at, he wouldn't come to us. We worked under the radar for obvious reasons.

"This has got to be related to the human trafficking operation that was on the news last winter," Boone said pensively.

I didn't watch the news, so I wouldn't know. "Why?" Human trafficking was as common as chlamydia, especially in Vegas.

"Because Darius was working that case," Boone replied. "I heard Ma and Aunt Mary talkin'. I didn't think about it, though. He's always off being a superhero somewhere."

Truth. Okay, so that explained that. We had no reason to dig further. A job was a job.

"Where do you wanna start?" I twisted my body to reach the side table next to the couch—or my makeshift nightstand, I guessed. I kept my weed in there.

"We need a list of priorities," he answered. Then he turned around to pop the window behind us. "Where does AJ live?"

"Up in Summerlin, of course." Where most of the rich fuckers lived. "He's got an estate in The Arbors. It's not gated, thankfully."

"So we'll get a tracker on his car...?"

I nodded and lit up a joint. "Who's— Fuck." I coughed at the first drag. Shit, way too dry. That's what I got for not smoking often anymore. The weed dried out. "Who's your best source at the Venetian?" Because we needed to see the reservation.

Combined with the Palazzo, the Venetian was the largest hotel complex on the Strip, so we had plenty of friends working there. I'd worked there myself too.

"I don't have anyone working the front desk at the moment," he replied with a frown. "I got Geoff in maintenance."

That was good. We might need him. "I'll call Laney." She worked behind the scenes in administration but had access.

After taking another drag, a more careful one, I held it in my lungs and handed over the joint to Boone.

He coughed a little too.

The sweet, pungent smell filled my senses, and my muscle memory kicked in before the weed did. Things slowed down a bit, shit was chill, and I didn't feel that underlying current that shot sparks of pain through me as soon as I laid eyes on my brother.

I exhaled and switched to an empty document.

"Soon as we get our hands on the reservation, we can start

connecting the dots and see if they've booked shit under other names, too." I began typing out some keywords and places where we could pick up clues. If they'd booked a whole block, they were gonna host quite the party. "I'll ask Willow if she can dig around to find airline tickets somewhere." The end of October was about six weeks away, meaning tickets should be booked already. If not for Lange himself, then at least the ones he wouldn't spring for private flights for. "Private airlines, car services," I mumbled to myself as I jotted it down. "See what kinds of comps they're looking at from the hotel. Dinner reservations, catering for the party venue, bar service..."

"We need a detailed floor plan too," Boone added.

I nodded along and added it to the list.

"Figure out the route between hotel block and venue," I muttered. "Get into AJ's house, map out his daily routine, look into his finances—maybe I'll ask Willow about that, too—and connect early arrivals linked to the family."

"Early arrivals?" Boone asked.

"If Alfred's traveling with heavy security, I'm banking on a crew arriving ahead of time to make sure everything's running smoothly."

"Ah. Yeah. Maybe you should sit down with TJ and get some ideas too. He'd know how these people get around."

He had a point. I made a mental note to call him later.

"Why's it always an AJ or TJ with these guys?" he mused.

I chuckled. "Right? Maybe it's some rule in organized crime —gotta have a bunch of juniors around."

We knew a DJ too, just as connected as TJ. They were cousins.

"Anyway," he drawled. "We do all this... What's in it for us?"

"I assume diamonds." I furrowed my brow in concentration

29

as I finished my list for now. "Darius said there'd be plenty of opportunities to get what we want from the target."

Boone let out a low whistle. "We like diamonds."

We sure did.

It was why I was extra keen on getting inside AJ Lange's estate. Alfred and his posse wouldn't travel with an abundance of valuables that weren't guarded day and night, but AJ would definitely keep some shit at home. Even if it wasn't diamonds or cash. We rarely went near art, because it was generally easy to trace, not to mention harder to sell. A woman's $500 shoes, though? The diamond studs in her jewelry box? The gold necklaces? A rich man's collection of golf clubs? Count us in. An estate like that—fucking gold mine. We weren't picky.

Just last year, a buddy and I made fifteen Gs selling stolen designer bags and suits.

"Here."

I glanced over my shoulder and accepted the joint he'd almost finished. Yeah, no wonder he looked high already. He'd been sucking that thing like a dick. Christ.

I pinched the joint between my index finger and thumb, and I took three quick hits before I had to put it out. "Let's talk gear," I croaked, holding my breath. "Do you have any fake identities you can still use in this town?"

Boone squinted and scratched his beard. "Uh, maybe three? Only one linked to a credit card—if you're thinking we gotta get a room at the Venetian."

I hadn't come that far, but good to know. "We'll circle back to that. I was more thinking it shouldn't be hard to get inside AJ's house through his cleaning service." And *all* rich folk had someone else doing their dirty work. "We'd get access if one of us took a job there."

He hummed. "Probably smarter to bribe someone who already works there, innit?"

He was right. I didn't know what I'd been thinking. "Good call." We didn't want cops around asking questions, which they would once Lange's estate had been robbed.

"I know. I've always told you, Case. You're the beauty, I'm the brains."

I barked out a laugh and opened my beer. "I'm the beauty *and* the brains. You're just the brawn."

He punched me in the arm, harder than he probably intended, and I hissed and rubbed the sore spot.

"Fuck you, I was trying to have a moment with you," he chuckled.

I took a swig of my beer, then smiled back at him. He was comfortable now, that was easy to see, all lounged back in his seat, one arm along the top of the couch, eyes a little glazed over.

I missed him.

How could I not? We'd always been there for each other. I'd been two or three when Mom adopted me. She and my biological mother had been childhood friends, having met in Sunday school or something else related to church back in the day. Aunt Mary had been there too, though she'd chosen another path. She'd met her soldier, Uncle James, and my mothers had left their little Irish Catholic bubble on the East Coast and decided to try their luck in Vegas.

They'd drifted apart when my biological mother went from being an average weekend warrior to getting into heavier drugs that she couldn't handle. Around the same time, Mom had given birth to Boone, and she couldn't cope with being a single mom, full-time worker, *and* making sure my biological mother didn't end up in a ditch somewhere.

She never did end up in a ditch. Instead, she dropped me off with Mom and Boone one day for a sleepover—I was about two, Boone had just turned three—and I was never gonna see the woman who'd given birth to me again. She overdosed that night.

I obviously had no recollection of it, but throughout my child-hood, Boone told me, "You're my brother now. I got you."

Toward the end of my twenties, we went through something similar again, and we were the ones who'd ended up with a toddler.

"Sometimes it feels like we've lived a thousand lifetimes together," I heard myself murmur.

Way too unfiltered. I hadn't meant to say that out loud. I cleared my throat and went for my beer again.

Fuck.

"Yeah," he responded quietly. "I just... I guess I didn't expect to wake up after my own funeral."

I swallowed and kept my gaze fixed straight ahead.

I supposed that was where we were now. Post-funeral. Two guys, two living dead, carefully testing the waters of a brother-hood that hadn't been resurrected.

"Fuck." I scrubbed a hand over my face. "I forgot how nostalgic weed makes me." It was just one of those things that'd gotten stuck. When we took on a new gig, we sat down and talked, smoked a joint, and made plans. "You wanna go get somethin' to eat?"

"Sure."

FOUR

"Time for bed, Aisley Paisley." I dove for her on our bed and peppered her face with kisses. "You're going to Gramma tomorrow."

"Yay!" she squealed.

It'd been a rough day. As if losing her mother hadn't dealt her the shittiest hand already, we'd said goodbye to her maternal grandfather today. Thankfully, our mother knew how to brighten Paisley's spirit with board games and too much sugar. She was good at explaining to a three-year-old about death, too.

"Are you ready to say goodnight?" I asked.

She yawned and crawled over to Case's side of the bed

where we'd placed a photo of Tia. Paisley kissed two fingers and brushed them against the picture, like we'd shown her, then crawled back to me.

"Pop-Pop's gonna sleep in heaven now?" she wondered. "Next to Nana?"

I nodded and pulled up the covers to her chin. "That's right. You can still see each other in your dreams."

"Hmm. Okay." She cuddled up next to me, and I took my cue and ran my fingers through her hair. "I don't remember Nana."

No, she'd died before Paisley was born. "Pop-Pop will introduce you," I murmured.

I caught Case standing in the doorway with a faint smile on his face.

Something settled within me, something I hadn't even known was shaky.

"Can you two sit still back there?" Boone asked exasperatedly. "The whole fuckin' van's shakin'."

Ace and I froze mid-dance move and shared a "Shit, we've been caught" look.

In our defense, stakeouts were boring.

"One more time, but we'll be still." Ace was ready to bargain.

"Can I be Barbie girl now?" I asked.

Boone snorted.

Ace hesitated. "I'mma be frank, Daddy. I don't think you can pull it off."

What the fuck?

"Sometimes you're not nice." I stole her soda bottle, which

made for a much better microphone than the Slim Jim I'd been forced to use. "Boone, push play again."

"Hold on. I think AJ's down for the night. Lights just went out."

Finally. We'd only been camped out down here on the street for two hours already. But at least we'd filled our bellies with pizza, and we were pretty comfortable in the back of the van. Plus, we had a cute dog wagging her tail whenever Ace and I goofed off.

It was probably a good thing we got this shit started soon. An unmarked van could only sit parked on a street lined with two-million-dollar homes for so long before someone became suspicious.

While Boone gave Ace her instructions again, I sang Aqua's "Barbie Girl" under my breath and moved to the beat in my head as I put the leash on the dog. When Ace had asked Mom's neighbor if she could watch their dog for a night, I bet they hadn't thought their shaggy little pup would be part of a master scheme. Ace had sounded so sincere too, claiming she wanted to use the dog to convince her daddies to get her one. And the elderly couple who lived in the house next to Ma's hadn't been able to resist her. They adored our girl, and who could blame them.

Speaking of neighbors... "How are we on the other houses?" I asked. Because it would look hella weird if, after being parked here for two hours, we were caught by a nosy neighbor watching us climb out to walk a dog.

"You're good," Boone said. "Lights are on straight ahead, but they can't see us."

"Aight, let's bounce."

He sighed heavily and looked back at me. "Are you ever gonna leave the '90s?"

I shot him a bitchy look in return and summoned my inner

Valley girl. "Talk to the hand." Then I glanced at Ace and made my way to the back. "Come on, baby. Time to commit a crime."

"Yeah. Cuz our faces aren't listening, Daddy." She flipped her hair over her shoulder, and Boone couldn't fight his amusement anymore.

I stepped out of the van first and set the dog on the ground. The street was dead, which was good. When the rich slept, the cat came out to play.

"Ewww, it licked me again." Ace wrinkled her nose and reluctantly accepted the leash. "I'm just...really more of a cat person. They don't get all up in my business." She waved a hand in front of her face.

I grinned at her.

After closing the door gently, I ushered her up on the sidewalk, and we started our little trek past one architect's dream after another. The houses all looked different, from older haciendas to modern, box-shaped structures. It was between two of the estates that Boone had kept AJ's house in sight, and as soon as we rounded a bend, we saw it too.

"There's a lesson to be learned here," I told Ace. "A house says a lot about the people who live there. What can you tell me about the man in that house?" I pointed toward AJ's estate.

Ace chewed on her lip and circled the dog's leash around her wrist. "He lives alone?"

He did, actually, and her conclusion impressed me. "What makes you think that?"

"Because it's gray and boring," she replied. "When you and Daddy were looking at the photos of the house online, it reminded me of Jen's dad's house." That would be a classmate's divorced parent. "He's got pebbles in front of the house instead of flowers, too, like this one. Just some cactus—but a *bunch* of spotlights. And boys love gadgets."

"You're fucking brilliant, Ace." I kissed the top of her head,

36

beyond proud. Not even nine years old, and she was so perceptive and aware of her surroundings. "You're right—it's a typical millionaire bachelor's home." Very modern. Polished steel and black flagstone met straight lines and the definition of minimalism. Two stories, slanted roof, infinity pool in the back, spotlights all over. As we got closer and passed AJ's neighbor, we got a quick glimpse at the back of the house. Only the pool was illuminated now. I couldn't see it clearly; there was a fence in the way, but the light shone through. "The problem with millionaire bachelors who love gadgets is that they probably love high security too. That's why we gotta be careful entering the premises. It wouldn't surprise me—since it's not a gated community—if he had motion sensors and camera surveillance."

Ace nodded thoughtfully.

"You ready?" I asked.

She quirked a brow. "Ready to look like a young child just walking her dog in the middle of the night to come off as incompicuous?" Oh, close enough.

"You're not supposed to know that word."

She rolled her eyes. "Whatever. I'm ready to be a prop."

Good. "For the record, dogs make sense of things. It's scientifically proven that you're less suspicious of someone walking a dog. If anyone saw us now, they'd draw the most innocent conclusions. A dad and worried daughter, walking their sick dog. That's why Daddy and I told you to wear your PJs." I side-eyed AJ's car in the driveway, deciding where to put the tracker. "Besides, we'll have a few errands around this house, so you wanna switch it up a bit. Tonight, it's you and me walking a dog. Next time, it might be Boone jogging—" I cracked myself up, and Ace giggled too. "Okay, that wouldn't happen, but you see what I mean? You don't wanna establish a pattern. People pick up on those."

With just a few feet to go, I retrieved the tracker from my

pocket and removed the protective film from the sticky underside. Ace took her cue and became a little more invested in the dog, and I discreetly slipped the tracker an inch or so behind the license plate.

"Yeah, you're such a good doggy, Daddy," Ace gushed as she patted the dog's head. "See what I did there?"

Yeah, I saw, freaking brat.

When she turned her head toward the house, I spoke up quickly. "Eyes ahead, baby."

"Right." She straightened again and kept walking. "Now what?"

"Now we continue walking our sick dog." I nodded up ahead. "We'll turn around at the end of the street and come back down on the other side."

"And then we return this smelly thing?"

I chuckled. "I'll return her tomorrow when you're struggling to stay awake in school."

"I'll keep a Red Bull in my locker," she replied flippantly.

The hell she would. "No, you won't. What kind of father would I be if I allowed that kind of poison?"

She squinted up at me. "Do you really wanna go there, Dad?"

I frowned. What?

"Love you, sweet pea. Dream of something cool." I pressed a kiss to her forehead before I made room for Boone to say goodnight.

"Night," she yawned.

I paused in the doorway to her room and watched Boone sit down on the edge of her bed. He was the best at tucking her in, she always said. I was better at story time.

"You're sleeping here too, aren't you?" Ace asked him. "It's too late for you to leave now."

Boone chuckled softly and grabbed her hand. "I can drive in the dark, believe it or not."

She wasn't satisfied with that response. "I'm just sayin'." Oh boy. "It would make your daughter very happy if her fathers could kiss and make up so we can be a family again someday. And live together."

Ouch. That one packed a punch.

"We *are* a family, baby," Boone insisted. "We make our own way, don't we?"

She huffed a little and turned onto her side, facing away from him.

I suppressed a sigh and ran a hand through my hair. Even if everything was good between Boone and me, how were we ever supposed to give her what she wanted? It made perfect sense for her to want her parents living together, but those parents were also brothers in our messy situation.

One day, Boone was gonna meet someone. Settle down, get married, maybe have another kid. I'd hopefully meet someone too. I just couldn't see it happening. Nothing that went beyond casual arrangements and short-term relationships. Four years of shoving Boone out of my life hadn't changed my feelings, so it was difficult to see a future where I got over him.

"Ace." Boone put a hand on her shoulder. "Come on, Aisley Paisley. You gonna send me off without a hug?"

Oh, for chrissakes. "You might as well stay tonight," I said. "It's three in the morning."

Boone glanced back at me with a fair amount of hesitation written across his features, and he would have to sort that out himself. The dog chose that moment to remind me of her presence, so I left the room and headed for the kitchen.

"Ace wanted to give you Red Bull," I told the dog, filling a bowl with water. "Remember that if you wake up and gotta piss. Her room's open." To showcase how nice I was, I even grabbed a few slices of turkey from the fridge. "Let's find you a spot, yeah?"

With the turkey and water in one hand, I grabbed a blanket from the couch and prepared the corner between the TV unit and the wall to the kitchen. Then I left her alone while she went to town on the turkey, and I threw the couch cushions on the floor and moved the coffee table. It was a good thing I'd bought a big couch so Boone could fit in there with me.

I sighed at the thought. How many nights had we spent together? How many nights had his brotherly and naturally affectionate personality fucking tortured me? He hadn't even seen the point in buying two beds when we'd lived together last time. Back then, Ace always ended up in the middle of the bed too. We'd wake up to her little feet padding across the floor. She delivered the same lie. Nightmare. Because she'd noticed Boone caved instantly when she'd had a bad dream.

Once I'd made the bed, I returned to the kitchen and switched on the oven to preheat. Middle of the night or not, I was hungry. Boone could probably eat too, so I grabbed the biggest frozen pizza that fit in my tiny freezer. Pepperoni and extra cheese with stuffed crust, fuck yeah. And a Pop-Tart or two while I waited.

When Boone emerged from Ace's room, I was trying to decide what flavor Pop-Tart I wanted. I had an entire cabinet just for them. Granted, it was a narrow corner cabinet, but I was still proud of my collection.

"I'm making pizza," I mentioned.

"If Pop-Tart came out with a pepperoni version, I ain't callin' it pizza."

I laughed and picked out the box with cinnamon roll flavor. "This is just as we wait. Want one?"

"Sure. Got any s'more flavored?"

"Got any s'more flavored," I scoffed. "Of-fucking-course I do. I keep blueberry around too." It was his favorite. I thought it tasted like medicine.

"If I say I'm flattered and a little touched, you're just gonna ruin it," he said.

I would never.

"It's no secret that you're a little touched, big brother." I popped the pastries, two of each, into the toaster, then turned around and leaned back against the counter.

He smirked wryly and leaned against the doorframe.

"Did you turn Ace's frown upside down?" I wondered.

He nodded with a dip of his chin. "Crisis averted."

"For now." Because this would come back at some point. "We'll have to talk to her sooner or later."

"We?" He hitched a brow. "How about *you* have that conversation with her? I was happy with us livin' together."

I frowned, both confused and annoyed. For one, he couldn't honestly see us sharing a home as a long-term solution. For two... "Why do you sound like a bitter ex?"

"Why do I feel like one?" He shrugged.

"Fuck if I know." I'd throw my arms out in frustration if I wouldn't hit them against the oven and the sink. My kitchen wasn't big. "At least with an ex, I'd have some memories of good sex to keep me goin'."

He snorted and folded his arms over his chest. "I don't know what to tell you. I thought we were on the same page. We were gonna work our asses off to get outta that shitty apartment and buy a house or something."

I swallowed uneasily. It was messed up how perfectly our dreams could align—and yet be worlds apart. "Sounds great and all," I muttered. "Until you find the woman you wanna start your own family with."

He let out a laugh. "Why do you sound like a bitter ex, Case?"

Because I fucking felt like one.

The Pop-Tarts saved me from responding, and I plated them before I told him to take them to the living room. I needed a minute. It was already becoming too much. Teaming up for gigs brought us so close, partly because we worked weird hours that often left us with long nights where we had nothing to do but shoot the shit, eat, talk about Ace, and just be with each other. And I wasn't sure I could go down that road again. Last time I'd cut all ties, I'd spent a week at the bottom of a bottle, and my anger had led me to take unnecessary risks at work. I'd stopped giving a fuck, which was dangerous. If I landed my ass in jail again and couldn't see my daughter, Jesus Christ, my life would be over.

"What kind of fucking pullout couch is this? It's comfier than most beds I've slept in."

I smirked to myself and placed the pizza in the oven. "The good kind that costs you two grand. Well, if you pay for it." After grabbing two sodas from the fridge, I left the kitchen for now. "Don't get crumbs in it, I fucking swear."

He was busy feelin' up my mattress. It was thick, solid, part memory foam, part soft like clouds.

"Figures..." An ounce of the bitterness seeped back. "First man I have in my new bed is my goddamn brother."

He flashed me a grin at that, a happy, pleased one that reached his eyes. Shit, I hadn't seen him smile like that in years. It was a slap in the face in a way, because I was more convinced than ever that he was suffering from some kind of depression.

I stripped off my jeans and pulled my tee over my head, then got in on the other side and reached for the remote on my nightstand. "Gimme my Pop-Tarts, and I will give you a couple episodes of *The Nanny*."

He chuckled. "I'll never get your obsession with the '90s. You know we have good shows now, too?"

They weren't bad nowadays, but they were no *Blossom* quality either.

I knew Boone and Ace had their own thing of watching DC and Marvel movies. He was her Joker; she was his Harley Quinn.

"I do watch new movies," I said in my defense. "I don't know. The '90s were just so...wholesome. Every comedy show is feel-good."

"You're the least wholesome guy I know, Case."

I quirked a smirk and bit into my Pop-Tart. "Maybe that's why I love it."

We all needed balance, didn't we?

Fucking hell, it was hot today.

As soon as Vegas bathed in triple digits, my systems started shutting down, and I craved air conditioning like some common tourist who'd never seen the sun.

I wiped my forehead and adjusted my shades, then glanced at the time. Any minute now. Taking a sip of my iced coffee, I eyed the woman in my rearview and hoped she didn't push my buttons today. Every motherfucking week I had Ace, I somehow ended up right in front of or behind the same woman. She had two boys to pick up and a schedule that probably had her crunching Valium like mad. Soccer, track, PTA, bake sales, golf, the whole nine yards. And if I didn't move my car in the pickup line exactly when the car ahead of me pulled forward, she honked at me.

My phone buzzed with a text, and I picked it up to see a message from Laney.

You got mail and a delivery. xxx

Fuck yeah. I was quick to text back.

I owe you dinner. Any place you want.

A message from Boone appeared before I could put down my phone again.

I returned the van and got the blueprints in a file. Want me to wait at Ma's?

"Hi, Daddy!" I heard Ace holler. I looked up at her quickly and saw I had a few seconds to spare as she ran toward my car, so I typed out a reply to Boone.

Picking up Ace now, gonna drop her off at Emma's. Go to my place and wait for me.

"Hey, baby." I tucked away my phone and reached over to open the door for her. "How was school?"

She didn't look tired at all, despite having been up so late last night. "It was good. Can you help me with my math assimament later?"

"Of course. I'll help you with your math assignment."

"That's what I said," she griped.

I stifled my mirth and peered ahead, then started the engine and backed up for as much as I could. The woman with her hawk eyes in the rearview perked up and waited for me to hit her or something, to which I flipped her off without looking back. With enough room, I was able to pull out and fuck off. AC on high.

"You eating at Emma's house?" I asked.

"I think so," she replied. "Her mom met someone who tries to impress her with a bunch of food."

"Hey, it works for Boone." I checked the rearview and switched lanes.

Ace laughed. "It's a chef! Emma says he comes over and cooks and stuff."

All right, then. Good for Emma's mom. Bella deserved it. Emma was the one friend of Ace's I really liked. They'd met a couple years ago when it was time for Ace to learn how to swim. The two were thick as thieves and shared similar personalities. The fact that they lived across town from each other hadn't stopped them from turning into best friends and hanging out as often as they could. It helped that Bella was a down-to-earth, balls-to-the-wall woman who took no prisoners. Whatever game Vegas threw at her, she changed the rules.

"Are you and Daddy working again tonight?" Ace asked.

"Yes, ma'am. No fun excursions, though. We'll be at home."

"Oh, poo. Fun escortions are fun."

I chuckled. "Excursions."

"That's what I said!"

FIVE

I had to do something about this obsessive need to check in with him. He was just at the store, for chrissakes.

He was noticing something was wrong too, wasn't he?

Fuck! There had to be something wrong with me. My jumbled thoughts threw fragments of solutions at me—that I wasn't sure were actual solutions. I was getting desperate. I couldn't meet anyone. Everything gave me doubts. It'd started when Paisley announced that she liked Case's new nickname for her. Ace. She wanted that to be her name. Then she'd stammered a little and asked what nicknames Case and I wanted, and we'd already known where that was going, because we'd told her we viewed her as ours. Our little *champion, our daughter. And the moment she'd called us her dads, everything outside my family had just faded away. Women, even friends—everyone stopped mattering to me. But my urgency to be closer to Case grew tenfold. As if Paisley had opened up a new world with two words. Dad. Daddy.*

Case was gonna get sick of me, though. He was already on edge these days, and I could see the signs because that used to be me. When ex-girlfriends had started getting clingy, I'd pulled away, feeling suffocated. Now I was doing the exact same shit with my own brother.

Except, I wasn't gay or anything. That was clear. I didn't eye men the way Case did.

The tension built up within me until my stomach hurt, and it wasn't released until I heard Case turning the key in the door.

He was home.

I exhaled.

Tonight, we were celebrating our daughter's fourth birthday.

The moment I walked through the door, three things struck me at once. Boone had tidied up and stowed away the bed, something from the kitchen smelled like pizza, and he was in the shower.

Talk about different from what I was used to.

Upon seeing a small cardboard box on the coffee table, I walked straight over there and picked it up. A courier from the Venetian must've been here already. I tore off the packing tape with their logo on it and sat down on the couch.

Soon I learned that I owed Laney a lot more than dinner.

I'd helped her get away from an abusive son of a bitch of a

boyfriend one time, and ever since, she'd gone above and beyond to help me if work brought me to her backyard on the Strip.

This time, aside from details about the reservation, I'd asked for insider tips that would give me a starting point from which I could get my hands on several things on my list, and it turned out she'd done most of it herself. I picked out several keycards, four ID tags, instructions, information about the suites, the housekeeping service's general schedule, some warnings and precautions I could take into consideration, and the reservation with all the details.

Last but not least, the employee information about the man from Hospitality that I needed to get close to at some point. He'd be in charge of the Langes' comfort during their stay, so he'd know all about preferences and comps.

A door opened down the hall, and I looked up just as Boone came out of the bathroom. *Oh, fuck you, big brother.* I'd forgotten this part about living with him. Shameless mother-fucker. Not that I possessed an ounce of shame either, but he wasn't queer. It didn't matter to him if I stepped out of the shower glistening wet with nothing but a towel around my hips.

He wasn't small anywhere. He was softness and power wrapped up in one. Defined pecs, biceps, broad shoulders, thick fucking thighs, a stomach made of steel...and then some cushion from the fast food he loved. Add the biggest heart, a charismatic grin, and blue eyes that sometimes flashed with the devil inside him, and...yeah.

There was no grin on his face now, though. As soon as he lowered the towel he'd used to run over his hair and beard, all I saw were bloodshot eyes.

I froze. We spotted each other at the same time. It was a fucking slap in the face, and it kept coming, pushing worry, the urge to protect, and nausea down my throat.

"What the hell happened to you?" I blurted out.

He swallowed and averted his gaze, and he sought out his jeans and beater next to the couch. "I didn't know you were home yet."

That...did not answer my question.

"Boone."

He sighed and stepped into his jeans. Oh, there goes the towel. Thanks. Just what I needed, his cock in my face. Or five feet away, whatever. "Just drop it," he said.

It fucked with my head to have his cock and balls on the forefront of my mind at the same time as I was worried sick. I had to shake my head and scrub my hands over my face. The hell was wrong with me? I'd seen him naked a million times before.

If he was a grower, God have mercy on the women who were lucky enough to get fucked by him, because he was a shower too.

"I knew something was wrong," I said. "My plan was to figure it out along the way, but now I'm just gonna ask. Are you depressed?"

"I told you to let it go," he snapped. Then he picked up his towels and returned to the bathroom.

"Because I'm so good at obeying orders." I didn't waste a second to follow him, but I stopped short when I almost walked into him as he left the bathroom again. He glared at me. For once, I didn't escalate anything. I didn't glare back or say anything bitchy.

"Get outta my way, Case," he warned quietly.

"No." I clenched my jaw. "You're gonna tell me what's wrong so I can fix it." I even grabbed his hand and gave it a squeeze to show I was ready to be his support animal through this. "I'm not going anywhere, Boone. I wanna know why you've been bawlin' your eyes out."

For some reason, that didn't work. He got angry and shoved

me aside, hard enough that I hit the wall with a thud. So I did what any normal person would do in my shoes. I jumped onto his back and latched on and demanded he tell me why he wasn't feeling well.

"The fuck is wrong with you?" he yelled.

"I'm showing you how much I care!" I hollered back. "Stop tryna push me off!"

He didn't. He rammed me into the kitchen doorway, and I cursed as fiery pain shot through my shoulder.

"I'm not letting go until you tell me," I snapped.

He let out a furious growl and stalked into the living room, and I tightened my arms and legs around him, anticipating he was gonna try to throw me off. Nice of him to do it over the couch, I guessed. Less nice that he sank his teeth into my arm.

"Motherfucker!" I shouted.

When the pain became too much, I felt my grip slipping, and he chose that moment to make a jerky motion over the couch that had me tumbling down. But in the last second, I managed to grab on to his beater, which ripped at the seams over his shoulders. The glare he gave me when my back hit the cushions was unearthly, and I saw his fist coming a mile away.

"Don't you—" I gnashed my teeth and got both my hands around his clenched fist.

He gave me the most condescending look, one which didn't require any translation. I got it. I was focusing all my strength on one single blow, and all he had to do was plant a knee between my legs and use his free hand to get me in a choke hold.

"You're dumber than you look sometimes," he sneered, chest heaving. "What're you gonna do now? You're just an annoying little insect."

"Fuck you," I spat out. "You can't swat me away."

"Looks like I can." He pressed me down a little harder, to the point where I had to refocus my efforts. I coughed and tugged on his arm. Blood rushed to my face, and fury set in. I had limits.

Hauling in a strained breath, I punched him in the gut and kicked against his thigh.

He cursed me to the pits of hell. In an attempt to immobilize my legs, he made the mistake of loosening his hold on my throat to get both his knees between mine, and I took advantage as quickly as I could.

I bitch-slapped the fucker right across his face.

Oh shit. Shit, shit, shit.

He'd been holding back before. I didn't stand a goddamn chance when he swiftly used his body to trap me against the couch, and he easily restrained my wrists over my head too. Unless I wanted to ram my forehead against his, I was out of options.

My lungs squeezed at the sheer mass of him pressing against me. Fuck me, I had fantasies that started out this way, only with less violence. Okay, sometimes with less violence.

He shifted on top of me, and it became impossible to switch gears once my brain dove for the gutter. Even though I hurt basically everywhere, all I could think of was that I hadn't been this close to him since we were fighting shit out like normal brothers in high school.

"You can only push me so far, Case," he said, out of breath. His low voice was full of threat. "If I don't wanna talk, I won't fucking talk."

A ball of nerves tightened my gut, and I flicked my gaze to his. So much anger and raw vulnerability swam in his eyes.

"I don't accept those terms," I rasped.

He chuckled darkly and peered down at our aligned bodies. "You're not in a position to make demands, little brother." Then he released one of my wrists and grabbed my jaw tightly, and before I could do fucking anything, he pushed harder against me, cursed under his breath, and slanted his mouth over mine.

The pure shock that bolted through me rendered me useless in a hot second. It didn't compute—any of it. He'd fucking fried my brain. This couldn't be happening. Maybe he'd lost it. That had to be it. He'd gone completely mental, and that was why he was currently swiping his tongue into my mouth.

Holy fuck, Boone was kissing me.

My body liquified underneath him as waves of heat rolled over me, but my mind was tinged with panic. Boone was straight. He wasn't feeling well. He did stupid shit sometimes, and I was the one who had to live with the regret later.

He stole a deep, sensual, hungry, desperate kiss that forced my surrender. I took an unsteady breath and slipped my hands free, then palmed his face and kissed him back tentatively.

He's gonna regret it soon, moron.

"Boone," I murmured hoarsely.

He wrenched away a few inches and stared at me unseeingly. He was so far away in his own world it wasn't even funny.

He swallowed hard and furrowed his brow.

"Talk to me," I whispered.

That brought him back. He sucked in a ragged breath and nearly flew off the couch.

Yeah, this was gonna blow.

I pushed myself up on my elbows and merely watched as he located his shirt, stuck his feet into his shoes, and patted his pockets for...I didn't know. Phone, keys?

"I gotta go," he muttered, never looking my way. Hurt slashed through me, but the worry won out. I had to give him some space.

He stalked out, maybe not even aware one of the wide straps to his beater was completely off, and I felt his departure in the foundation of the trailer. Every step.

I blew out a breath and sat up.

The timer in the kitchen buzzed.

So I guessed the pizza was ready.

Maybe I'd accidentally switched off notifications...

I reached for my phone and brought the screen to life, but no, still no response from my brother.

Fuck. I dreaded to think what he was going through. At least he was at Mom's place. He wasn't alone.

"Daddy, are you dying?" Ace asked.

I tapped my pen against my lip and glanced back at her in question.

She nodded at the TV. "Niles said something funny, and you didn't laugh."

Oh. Well, I could blame work. I cleared my throat and motioned vaguely at my laptop, the three notepads, printouts, and one iPad I had on the coffee table. "Just distracted by work."

She hummed and slid forward on the couch. "Can I help?"

I mustered a small smile and picked up a stack of printouts and the yellow highlighter. "You can go through these documents and look for the name Jin Yu." I spelled it out for her too. "Whenever you see it in the list, mark it."

"Like in *Clueless*!" Ace said triumphantly.

I grinned. "Exactly like in *Clueless*. You know how to make a father proud, baby."

She smiled in satisfaction and got straight to it.

I went back to worrying about Boone and cataloguing AJ Lange's driving route today on my iPad. The man went to work early. At six-thirty, he'd pulled into the offices of the Nevada Gaming Control Board, and I was Jack's complete lack of surprise to discover he worked in the Enforcement Division.

Corrupt motherfucker.

Well, if investigating organized crime was this criminal's job, I might as well contact TJ right away.

I grabbed my phone—still no text from Boone—and sent my buddy a message through the usual app we used. No risk of any nosy fuckers seeing.

Oi. Got time to meet up soon? I have some questions about an AJ Lange at the NGCB.

He usually replied quickly. Despite being some ten years younger than me, that guy was hungry to climb ranks and lived and breathed work.

I sent another text to Boone while I waited.

You can't shut me out completely. I'm worried about you. I swear I'm not reading into what happened earlier. I've done stranger things at low points in my life, you know that. Just talk to me.

I'd barely pressed send before TJ's response popped up in three quick messages.

Oh, that fuckin guy.
Sure. When?
I have time tomorrow and Sat.

Tomorrow could work. It was Friday. Boone's week with Ace, so he or Mom would pick her up after school.

Tomorrow, usual place. 3pm?

TJ and I met up at a diner on the outskirts of town the following day. The place was dead. People hadn't gotten off work yet, and the lunch crowd was long gone.

"It's been a minute, my man." He slapped his hand into mine. "How's life?"

"Killing me," I chuckled. "How's the family?" All two hundred of them. TJ and his family had been here since the '70s, and they'd...made themselves known in their Italian-American way, so to speak. You couldn't really live a life in the underworld and not know of his family, even today.

He widened his eyes and slid into the seat across from me. "Killing me, of course. It's what they do."

I smirked and flipped open the menu.

When the waitress came over, we ordered some sliders and shakes—best strawberry shake in all of Nevada—and then got down to business.

"So you got beef with Lange or what?" he asked.

I shrugged, not wanting to get into detail. "I guess I wanna know how secure his future is with the Commission."

He snorted. "Too secure, in my opinion. His work protects him, and he's in the pocket of some mameluke down in Florida."

I nodded once. "His pop."

We halted our conversation as the waitress returned with our shakes.

It must've been some sight, two grown-ass men living on the wrong side of the law sucking strawberry milk shakes from straws with a swirly design. But we owned this shit. Well, to each other. No need to tell others.

"Listen," he said. "I'm not gonna ask what your plan is. But if getting rid of Lange is the goal because you got personal issues with him, my best bet would be to pin somethin' on him. Right now, his record is spotless—always has been. Because the Board knows of his biological affiliations. Which means, you know, he's gotta watch his back and constantly be the golden boy. Smallest suspicion from the higher-ups, and he's done. That's my two cents."

I nodded slowly, thinking, and the truth was, I didn't know

exactly what Darius's plan was. It didn't matter to me. He'd asked me to find out as much as possible about Lange, that's all.

"You don't seem like a fan of him either," I noted.

He chuckled. "Fuck no. But they're all the same to us. If we get rid of one, another takes his place." He shrugged. "I'll admit, AJ's in a league of his own because of the pressure he's under. He works around the clock to shut down any casino-related business that has so much as a typo on the permit. But at the end of the day, you gotta pick your battles, and a lot has changed just in the past twenty years. We don't really deal in gambling anymore."

I knew that much. I'd lived through some of those changes myself. Vegas would probably always have a lot of crime, though it'd shifted to a smaller scale. It wasn't a town run by the mob anymore.

Unless you counted politicians...

SIX

"Sweetie, I'm sure you'll work things out." Mom stroked my back while I kept my face hidden against the back of her couch.

Christ, I'd fallen apart.

It was a good thing Ace wasn't with me.

The pain was crippling. I still saw his face every time I closed my eyes. I saw the raw hurt in his expression, then the anger that'd followed. The sheer rage.

"You're dead to me, Boone. You're fucking dead to me."

I swallowed hard against a new round of emotions and screwed my eyes shut.

"Can I stay here awhile, Ma?" I croaked. "Case is moving out of the apartment, and I can't afford the rent on my own."

"Oh, of course, baby. Stay as long as you need."

I didn't even care how pathetic it made me. I was too consumed by the loss of the center of my universe.

———

I squinted past the sleep in my eyes and read Boone's message half a dozen times.

Several years ago, you made me promise never to hook up with anyone around you. I didn't understand why, and you refused to explain. I broke that promise three times, never seeing the big deal, and then you cut me out of your life. I've been living with that regret ever since, and sometimes it becomes too much. I'm not depressed, Case. It's just grief. I'm not coping well without you.

I gotta ask something selfish. I need this job. I need the payout so I can start over and afford a place for me and Ace. But before we see each other again, I want your word that we won't speak of what happened yesterday. I'm embarrassed as fuck, and you're not exactly the smoothest guy to make things less awkward. I can't explain right now anyway.

"Ugh." I dropped my phone, and my head hit the pillow again.

If the sun wasn't up, neither was I.

That used to apply to Boone too, yet he'd sent this at four in the morning.

I was so fucked. All the distance I'd put between us, the

armor I'd hammered into place—all of it—just disintegrated into the tiniest of fragments. No panic or dread. I was just resigned to do whatever it took to make him feel better, and that included telling him why I'd begged him to make me that promise all those years ago.

Fuck. I could already feel my head spinning. I wasn't gonna be able to get back to sleep, so I might as well call him.

I grabbed my phone again and clicked on his number. Then I rolled onto my back and blinked sleepily.

"Why are you up this early?" was how he answered the call.

I yawned. "Been on pins and needles to hear back from you." The faintest vibration from my phone had captured my attention instantly since he'd walked out of here.

"You could've just texted that I have your word," he said.

I could've.

"I'mma tell you something first," I murmured drowsily. I knew just where to begin, too, because it'd been on my mind a lot lately. "You remember that we always went to Giordano's for pizza after a gig. *I* remember that we usually hit up a club afterward, and it never took many drinks before you had some bunny in your lap. And if you *think*, Boone, you can figure out why I didn't wanna see you with anyone."

For years after I figured out I was drawn to him, it still wasn't a problem to see him with a chick, partly because it never seemed serious, and partly because I'd been thinking with my cock at the time. I was too busy making rounds in the gay community. But then one time in Reno, I'd walked in on him screwing Tia, Ace's mom. A few years before she'd been born. And I'd fuckin' lost it. Completely flipped my shit. Because it was suddenly serious. My position as Boone's closest friend and brother-in-arms was threatened, 'cause we worked a lot with Tia. We teamed up often and became very close. She was the perfect decoy when we robbed old rich guys blind.

I'd made it about work. The rage I hadn't been able to contain, I blamed on work. I said it was fucking stupid to jeopardize our focus by getting laid while we were working together. They thought I was overreacting, that it was nothing, that it was just sex, no strings, no attachment—didn't matter to me. I couldn't unsee them. The jealousy had blazed through me, and I'd known I was beyond screwed.

It was the first time I'd asked him to promise me never to bring a woman around when I was nearby. I just couldn't stomach watching it.

Once we'd cooled off, he'd agreed, without understanding why it mattered that much to me.

"No, I can't figure it out," Boone said after a moment's silence. "I've fuckin' tried, Case."

Could he be that blind? Nearing the end, when I'd felt myself approaching my breaking point, I hadn't been subtle. I'd been downright possessive of him. I'd lied in order to spend more time with him too—away from others. He'd suggested a bar; I'd told him I wasn't feeling too hot and that we should stay in and watch movies. He'd invited me to a party; I'd derailed him with an out-of-the-blue trip to LA because he loved going to the beach. He'd proposed a gig with some woman he'd fucked in the past; I'd made up a bullshit excuse about it being too risky.

The jealousy had festered to the point where I'd felt genuinely ill.

"Try harder," I replied quietly. "If a woman told you not to see another woman, you'd suspect jealousy, wouldn't you?"

I heard him opening the patio door in the background. A beat later, I heard the flick of a lighter being lit. It wasn't often he smoked cigarettes, and Ma wouldn't allow weed at home.

"You're not some woman," he said.

"Astute observation, big brother."

Every other time I'd thought about coming clean to him, I'd

been filled with panic. Now, nothing remotely close to it. My breaths came out steady, my pulse wasn't spiking, nausea wasn't crawling up my throat.

I guess, in a way, I'd run out of things to lose. Only Ace mattered as much as Boone's well-being. The rest was secondary.

"Case..."

He got it now, didn't he?

I swallowed. Nervousness flared up and rattled around, but I could live with that.

"The last time really fucking hurt." I stared up at the ceiling and couldn't stop the memories from four years ago from rushing back. "You did that on purpose." They hadn't even been screwing. I'd been working late, Ace had spent the night at Ma's place, and I'd come home to find Boone getting head on the couch from a downstairs neighbor.

Good times.

He'd known exactly when I was due home.

"Jesus Christ." His voice sounded raw, like he'd been chain-smoking for fifty years instead of one smoke every now and then. "I wish I'd known, Case. I was... Fuck. I was dealing with my own shit back then, and I wanted to make sure you didn't think— I don't know. My head's a mess. And I guess it's been a mess for a while."

Make sure I didn't think what?

"I'm sorry I hurt you," he murmured. "I'm sorry I lost you."

Those words packed a punch harder than I was equipped to deal with right now. I didn't wanna dwell. In fact, I was suddenly itching to change the topic. I'd told him the truth. It was out there now. Maybe if he understood me better, we could figure shit out.

"You didn't lose me permanently," I said, clearing my throat. "We'll find a way that works for both of us, okay? I want you to feel better—that's my priority." I paused and decided we'd had enough of the heavy now. I didn't like getting all serious. "Breakfast is another priority. When you're done moping because you stuck your tongue down your brother's throat, swing by with food. I want two Sausage McMuffins and two hash browns."

———————

Thank fuck we had a lot to do in the days that followed, because Boone's transformation was so instant it nearly gave me whiplash. He was cracking jokes again. His batteries were charged. He smiled more. And he was determined that we'd "find our way back to each other." His words.

I also caught him studying me sometimes, and I didn't like it. It felt like the obvious question was on the tip of his tongue. The one where he asked if I still harbored those feelings for him.

So far, he'd steered clear of any topics that might be sensitive, probably because he knew that if he prodded, I would do the same, and he didn't wanna discuss the day that'd ended with him kissing me.

To be honest, neither did I. We'd finally found a common ground where we could work and hang out together without hostility in the air, and I wanted to savor that.

"Hey, Mac."

"You again," he chuckled.

I smirked and planted my laptop on the top counter he sat behind, day in and day out. Well, when he wasn't out in the trailer park playing handyman.

"You know the drill," he said.

I nodded and connected my laptop to his printer via Bluetooth, and I hit print on all seventeen pages. Then I fished out my wallet and did advanced math in my head. One quarter for each printout.

I slapped a five on the counter. "You got any single-wides for sale these days?"

He looked up from his computer. "'Fraid not. Just two doubles. Why, you not happy with your lot?"

"It's for my brother. He's looking for a place." Or he would be, once this job had paid off.

I wouldn't mind having him close. It'd make shit a lot easier for Ace too.

"I'll let you know as soon as something opens up," Mac replied, giving me my change.

"Thanks, man." I closed my laptop again and walked over to the printer on the side of the front desk. After collecting the printouts and quickly clearing the printer history, I walked out of the office again and checked the time on my phone.

We had a couple hours left before Boone was picking up Ace from school, and then we had some special plans we hoped would make our girl's day.

I jogged up the steps to my newly painted porch and noticed Boone had stowed away the seat cushions to the chairs while I was at the front office.

"Yo," I said, entering the trailer. "I'm ready to lay the puzzle."

Boone emerged from the kitchen with two beers and a bag of pretzels. "I put the tape on the TV."

Great. Together, we started attaching the printouts to the wall next to the TV. It helped to have the bigger picture right in front of us, literally. Twelve pages made up the floor plan of the room block the Langes had reserved for their stay. Twenty-eight suites on the forty-fifth floor of the Palazzo tower.

The remaining printouts were of the junior ballroom they'd booked.

I took a step back, folded my arms over my chest, and chewed on my thumbnail.

Something wasn't adding up.

"What's wrong?" Boone asked.

"This can't be all of it," I replied.

"Because the ballroom seats more guests than they've booked rooms for?" he guessed. "They're probably only springing for suites for the closest."

No, that part made sense. "It's not that. Look at the suites. They're all the same." It was their standard luxury suite. "No matter how much I love Mom, she'd be in a regular room while I grabbed the honeymoon suite if I ever got married."

Boone frowned. "No one's getting married, Case. It's a birthday celebration."

I waved that off as semantics. "Same principle. Alfred Lange is supposedly the head of this huge crime organization, and it's his birthday. I can't imagine him staying in the same kind of suite as the rest of the inner circle. Either we're missing something—maybe there's a penthouse suite booked under a different name, I don't know—or Alfred and his wife aren't staying at the hotel at all."

Boone furrowed his brow at the floor plan and mirrored my stance.

Hopefully, we'd get some answers tonight. We were meeting up with Laney for dinner at the Venetian at eight, and she was bringing a friend—namely, the woman who'd been assigned to assist the Langes with their party planning.

I needed clues.

According to Laney, the woman had a thing for tatted, mysterious bad boys, so I guessed I was gonna pretend to be straight tonight. And mysterious. And bad.

I should clue Boone in on that. "By the way, we're doing some role-play tonight," I said, keeping my stare fixed on the floor plan. "I gotta be available to that woman Laney's bringing. She's into elusive bad boys."

"Who're gay?" he asked without missing a beat.

I chuckled and clapped him on the back. "I won't be gay tonight." I could tell he wasn't satisfied with the response, which led me to believe he was wondering why I didn't just tell him to do the role-play. And I didn't want him to think it had anything to do with jealousy, because it seriously didn't. "I would've told you to do it if it wasn't for the fact that you can't act elusive to save your life. You may look like a bad boy, but we all know you're the family teddy bear who's nicer than Santa."

"Santa ain't fuckin' nice. He spies on people, keeps lists, and denies kids presents if they're not livin' up to his standards."

I grinned at him and shook my head. "Only a nice guy like you would point that out, so case closed."

He huffed, then muttered under his breath. "I can be elusive."

Sure, sure.

"So what're we telling Ace?" he asked.

I shrugged and scratched my arm. "I don't think we have to tell her a whole lot. We'll just let her know that I'll be trying to catch that woman's interest in order to get information."

If there was one thing Ace loved, it was to "work" with her daddies, even if only for the moment. Ma would have to stand in as babysitter sooner or later.

"Oh my gosh, this is so exciting!" Ace squealed behind her hands. "Wait, he's gonna open the door for you, Daddy."

I smiled and stepped out of the cab, then extended a hand to Ace.

"Welcome to the Venetian, sir. May we assist you with any luggage?"

"All good, thanks. We're traveling light," I replied.

The starstruck look in Ace's eyes as she looked up at the lights in the valet bay of the resort made my day. She'd been here before, more than once, but never as a hotel guest. When we'd told her we were spending the night, she'd lit up like a Christmas tree.

The three of us cleaned up good when we wanted to. Both Boone and I had donned dress pants and proper shirts, and Ace was sporting a classy black dress and had a bow in her hair.

I'd stolen a moment earlier back home when I'd stood in the kitchen doorway and watched Boone help her with her hair. Him in those charcoal pants that made his ass look like...*fuck me*. The pale gray fabric of his shirt stretching around his muscular arms... Ink peeking out from under his cuffs and collar. An affectionate smile at Ace's animated rambling about something, all while he tucked a piece of hair that'd come loose back into the hairband and adjusted the cute bow *just so*.

Those memories were my favorite.

The three of us made our way inside the hotel, Boone carrying our only bag, and Ace got in between us and grabbed our hands. She gazed up at the high ceiling and marveled at the luxurious design. I couldn't remember if she'd been in this area of the resort before, but it was impressive for someone who'd been here a hundred times over the years, too.

Even as a resident, as someone who'd grown up in this town, I found the hotels and casinos along the Strip a bit magical. If I was just driving from one side of town to the other, I did everything in my power to avoid this part, and I loathed the tourists who couldn't drive, but...yeah. Coming here from time to time, to eat, to gamble a little, to have a good time, was a treat.

We went through check-in without a hitch, and I gave them a credit card with a name that matched the one Laney had put on the reservation. I wasn't born yesterday. No matter how innocent our stay was, I knew what kind of privacy policy these places had. In a hot second, your personal information could be available to third parties in other countries where they gave no shits about integrity.

Cash was king. So was making reservations through friends or over the phone. The internet was only a great tool if you knew how to use it. Otherwise, it was a digital fingerprint.

"You remember our rules for the Strip, baby?" Boone asked Ace as we headed for the elevators.

People everywhere—Christ. These hotels were more like their own towns. The Venetian alone had over six thousand suites, several pools, lounges, and nightclubs, two massive floors packed with shops and restaurants, around twenty ballrooms, and every detail was Italian extravagance.

"Duh," Ace replied, skipping into an empty elevator. "Someone's always paying attention. Definitely no shoplifting."

I laughed.

We went up to the forty-fifth floor, and Boone and I got out our phones. He was to take pictures of everything, and I was gonna record a video.

Despite the heavy security, most hotels actually had very little surveillance on the hotel floors. If any at all. The Venetian didn't.

"Get behind us, sweet pea," I instructed. "By the way, did you turn off your phone?"

"Yes, sir. I ain't accepting The Man's cookies, and he can't take my geographic data and biology information."

I smiled, damn proud of her.

So was Boone. "You're gonna go far, you know that? And I think you mean geolocation and biometric information."

"That's what I said."

I kept my amusement to myself and trailed down the corridor toward our room, stopping briefly at emergency exits and maintenance spaces to record for Darius.

In just a few weeks, this floor would be flooded with human traffickers and murderers.

Opening the door to our suite, I wondered who would stay in here. Maybe a rapist? An inner circle security guard? A hit man?

The door closed behind me, and I peered into the luxurious bathroom and had a feeling Ace would want a bubble bath before we checked out. She'd have dinner with us, and then Ma would come watch her for a few hours while Boone and I tried to get our hands on information. Solid plan, I thought.

Christ, rich people couldn't even have the toilet in the same room as the bathtub—it had to be in its own little space.

Past the entryway was the bedroom area, taken up mostly by an oversized king bed.

An actual railing divided the suite, and I stepped down in the sunken living room area where a big L-shaped couch, table, desk, and entertainment unit sat. Not to mention a spectacular view of the Strip. I filmed it all, just in case Darius wanted video of the inside too. By the time I was done, Boone came in with Ace.

"Oh my God!" Ace was in love, evidently. "Look how big the bed is, Dad!"

She jumped up on the bed and declared it the best in the world.

Boone walked my way and said he'd taken pictures of everything.

"Perfect." I'd send it all to Willow tomorrow. "Ace, did you see the bathtub?"

She instantly flew off the bed and darted into the bathroom.

"You haven't once mentioned any expenses. We're supposed to split those." Boone glanced around us before his gaze landed on the impressive view. "How much was this room for a night?"

I shrugged. "Laney got us a 40% discount."

"That's not what I asked."

I raked my teeth across the corner of my lip and scratched my eyebrow. "You said you were short."

"Not on cash for—you know, this kinda shit. I still have my buffer. I just can't afford a good place to live yet. I'm done with roach-infested apartments and shacks that are one Santa Ana wind away from fallin' apart." He folded his arms over his chest, visibly determined. "I want a nice house for Ace to grow up in."

I couldn't help but get defensive. "What's wrong with the way I live? She has her own room. We go to the pool sometimes. I take her wherever she wants to go."

"And your neighbor has a meth problem."

"He moved out! He got arrested. He's not there anymore."

He rolled his eyes at me. "You know what I mean, Case. Don't tell me you're planning on spending the rest of your life at that trailer park. There's a reason you haven't sold off the gold bars from that stunt we pulled in Lake Tahoe six years ago. You're saving up for something."

Damn Mom for tattling.

I didn't know exactly what I was saving for, only that college and houses were pricey.

"Ladies?" a suspicious voice asked behind us. "You're not fighting, are you?"

We turned around and faced our daughter, and it was hard not to smirk at the little shit. She tried to look all demanding and ready to scold us, hands on her hips, eyebrow cocked.

"Does that sound like something we would do?" Boone walked over to her and quickly scooped her up, and without much difficulty, bunched up her dress to blow raspberries on her stomach. "Huh? Answer me, Aisley Paisley. Does that sound like something we would do?"

She wailed with laughter and tried fruitlessly to shove him away.

I checked my watch.

"Guys, we have an hour till dinner," I said.

Ace gasped through a laugh while Boone continued his assault. "I wanna shop! I wanna go where they give you pretty—gah, stop it, Daddy! Pretty, pretty paper bags instead of plastic bags."

She sounded like Ma. She felt special when she went to the outlet mall and they handed her whatever she'd bought in one of those boutique-type of bags instead.

"Then we should get going." I walked past them and brushed my hand up Boone's back. "Yo. Tickle monster. Let's bounce."

"All right." He chuckled, out of breath, and helped her straighten her dress. "Lemme just put the beers and sodas in the fridge."

I didn't know he'd brought any, but I loved him for it. Fuck minibar prices.

A few minutes later, we were back in one of the elevators, and I got stuck on the reflection of us in the doors.

"Look at us," I said. "We're the best family."

Ace grinned goofily and stuck out her tongue.

Boone draped an arm around my shoulders. "Damn right. Didn't know you'd gotten fancy, though. Is that a real Armani belt?"

I looked down and adjusted the narrow buckle. "Fancy...?" I wasn't sure a belt qualified as making someone fancy. "It's my lucky belt for special occasions." I flashed Ace a wink in the elevator door.

She beamed smugly.

"Special occasions," Boone snorted. "I know what that means. For when you score on dates. It ain't *that* nice."

"What the fuck?" I scowled at him.

"Yeah, what the fudge, Dad!" Ace demanded and spun around on us. "It was a gift from Gramma. *I* helped her pick it out!"

He'd for sure stepped in a big pile of shit now. But I suddenly had a greater concern, and it took no effort to ignore Boone's wince of regret.

"Since when do you say *fudge*?" I asked Ace, baffled and, to be honest, a little worried. We weren't the type of family that kiddified words.

Ace didn't struggle with the swift topic change, and she walked out of the elevator backward as soon as the doors opened. "I just felt like I'd reached my quota for the day. That's what Gramma says sometimes. It means there's a pacific number of times you can curse every day."

"Hear that, Boone?" I nudged him with my elbow. "There's a pacific number."

"Well, I don't wanna know it." He planted his hands on Ace's shoulders and turned her around. "Let's get this little doll-face some overpriced shit that comes in a nice bag."

"If you admit that Daddy's belt is pretty," Ace said.

I quirked a brow at Boone, waiting.

"It's very pretty," he conceded. "I was just fuckin' with him."

No, he hadn't been.

SEVEN

"You ever wonder why we never bother inviting you to parties and clubs anymore?" Jay asked.

I finished my whiskey and nodded at the bartender. Time to close my tab. "Not really."

Jay sighed and slid off his barstool. "I'll tell you anyway. It's because you're dead. Think about that while you pay for my beer. I gotta take a piss."

I scowled at his retreating form, then reached into my back pocket for my wallet.

Maybe I was dead. Today, it certainly felt like it. It was Casey's week with Ace, and it happened to be her eighth *birthday. I wouldn't get to celebrate her until this weekend, and it fucking sucked.*

"Hi."

I side-eyed the woman who sat down next to me.

She was shopping for a lay; that much was clear.

"Don't waste your time on me," I said.

She pursed her lips for a beat, undeterred. "What if I don't see it as a waste?"

New approach, then. "Don't waste my time either," I drawled. "I ain't interested." I hadn't been, for years. Couldn't even remember the last time I got laid or even fooled around with someone. It was before my brother had cut me out of his life.

Jay was right. I was a dead man.

"I wanna do more of this," Boone murmured.

I smiled at Ace, watching as she walked around the little accessory shop. It was best Boone and I stayed right outside; we had a way of breaking shit.

"Yeah." So did I. I just had to be careful, because this was one of those moments that made me wanna play "Kiss Me" by Sixpence None the Richer on repeat.

Having Boone as my brother was already difficult. Having a daughter with him...? Whole other circle of hell. Because he was never just one guy. There was the loving douchebag who could beat me physically and poke fun, the typical brother, both a jackass and a protective friend. Just like I was to him. That was the guy who hugged me hard for my birthday, smacked me good-naturedly upside the head in a quick "good job" or "I got you." But as co-parents, something constantly caused us to blur the lines. Not counting the four years we'd avoided each other.

Be it a rough day when Ace was in a shitty mood and we just needed a long hug, or a game day when she'd scored a lot and Boone and I spent all night talking to each other about how fucking awesome she was. Or right this second, when we watched our girl grow up before our eyes and Boone threaded our fingers together and squeezed my hand.

I had mad respect for parents who raised their kids all alone, because I wasn't sure how I'd cope. I couldn't imagine not having Boone around to share this with. After all, he was the only one who got it. Nobody else, without a claim, without loving her the way we did, would ever understand, because you cared to this extent about your own kids, not others'. In fact, I couldn't give two shits about other people's kids. They annoyed me.

Even during these past four years, we'd had a handful of moments where we could at least meet in the middle and be proud as parents. There was no off-switch to that need.

The problem for me was how we manifested that love as parents. It could too easily be misinterpreted. Him taking my hand because it was a sweet moment to see Ace all dolled up trying to pick out a bracelet...? It was intimate, no matter the intention, and it was bringing back all the feelings I'd worked twenty-four seven to bury.

"I think we're due for a family vacation," I said.

Ace had wanted to go on a Disney cruise since she'd learned how to talk.

I saw Boone's smile at the corner of my eye.

"Fuck yeah." He gave my hand another squeeze before he let go and entered the store. "Did you find anything, Ace?"

I blew out a breath and checked the time. Fifteen minutes till dinner. We were close to the indoor plaza where the canal with the gondolas ran through, not to mention a million more shops and restaurants.

Ace had moved on to a display of what looked like pins, which explained why she looked like a pig in shit, and she held up one to show Boone and whispered something in his ear. Knowing her, she'd buy a few.

She was too cute. She'd gotten a couple "pretty paper bags" already. A pink one with gold handles from a shop where she'd bought bath bombs and soap that glittered, and a signature Venetian bag from a gift shop where she'd bought a few souvenirs.

Boone was right. She deserved more of this. She never asked for much, just us being together, living under the same roof, spending time as a family. And Boone and I weren't a divorced couple where such a living arrangement wasn't possible; we were brothers. I considered the hatchet already buried, and we should be able to find a way to coexist. For her.

When Boone and Ace walked out again, she'd gotten her third pretty paper bag, and she could not look more pleased.

"I bought you a gift, Dad!" She skipped over to me and dug a hand into her bag.

"You did? That's sweet of you." I grinned as I noticed Boone attaching a pin to his shirt. It was a slice of pizza. Fucking perfect. And not even putting on a tux would stop him from wearing it.

"Because you love your iced coffee." Ace extended her hand and opened it, revealing a pin of a white to-go cup. It had a pink paper sleeve and the word "princess" written on it.

I laughed and hugged her to me. "I love you, you little shit."

"I thought it was fitting," Boone drawled, his eyes glinting with mirth. "You're our princess."

I made a *fantastic* princess. Boone may be the one who could braid hair, but I had a strong nail polish game.

"Help me put it on," I said and got down on one knee. Ace

giggled and handed over her bags to Boone before she took the pin from me and attached it to my shirt.

Boone took out his phone and snapped off a picture of us. "Ace, show Daddy the pin you got for yourself."

"In a second..." She was concentrating. "There!" With my new pin in place, she took a step back and smiled widely. "It looks perfect, I think."

"I think you're right." I leaned forward and puckered my lips, and she gave me a loud smooch before I stood up again. Then she dug out her own pin to show me, and I chuckled. It was a rainbow resting on two sparkly clouds that read "Fuck Off."

"I found a typewriter pin for Gramma, too," she added. "She says she's almost done with her novel."

Oh, it'd been almost done for about two years now.

"You're a sweetheart." I touched her cheek. "You ready to go eat? We gotta be at the restaurant in a few minutes."

She nodded and reclaimed her shopping bags. "Yeah, I'm hungry. Some food and calling in sick from school tomorrow would definitely help."

Boone and I cracked up.

"That was slick," he laughed.

Legit.

There would be no calling in sick. However, Boone had informed the school that she'd arrive late because of a dental procedure, so we had time. We weren't leaving until checkout at eleven.

This night was gonna suck. It was great to see Laney again, but after our short shopping spree with Ace, I wanted to crawl back into my family moment, not be at some swanky Italian place where I had to pretend to be interested in a woman named Alex.

We'd barely gotten past introductions, and she already bugged me. Partly because I couldn't find a single flaw in her. She seemed perfectly nice. She was beautiful, too. Big brown eyes, a dimpled smile, cute nose, wavy dark hair—she screamed of warmth and a bit of mischief. Like Ace.

So of course I had to hate Alex a little bit, because my brother couldn't take his eyes off her.

Laney came back from the hostess desk, having asked how long our wait would be for a table, and she looked a little flustered. Big crowds weren't her jam; I knew that much. It was why she preferred to work in an actual office and not anywhere near the hotel guests.

"Another ten or fifteen minutes," she said over the din.

I put a hand on her lower back, then gestured to a table in the corner of the bar. "Go have a seat. Boone and I will get us some drinks. Whiskey sour, right?"

She smiled gratefully and tucked a piece of her blond hair behind her ear. "Yes, please. Alex likes wine and cider. I'll watch Ace."

I dipped my chin, then motioned for Boone to follow me.

We made our way to the circular bar in the middle of the floor, and I ordered beer for Boone and myself, a whiskey sour for Laney, a glass of white for Alex, and a soda for Ace.

He leaned in close and spoke in my ear. "You can't go through with the act."

I frowned at him at the same time as a fucker behind me bumped me closer to my brother. I sent the idiot a warning look before I turned back to Boone.

"Why not?" I asked.

"Because her real name isn't Alex," he replied. "I don't

know why she's working here under a different name, but that's Allegra Colucci."

Shit. *Shit.*

TJ and DJ's cousin. Why the fuck...? I didn't get it. "That doesn't make any sense," I managed to get out. My mind started spinning, and a bunch of things I'd picked up over the years came back to me. For starters, TJ's family was several decades behind and would never allow a woman to work with anything illegal. And why else would the chick take another name? Then I thought about her age. I'd briefly noticed that *Alex* looked to be on the young side—for a hot second, I'd been impressed by her ambition to land a position like that at the Venetian in her early twenties. But considering she was objectively beautiful as fuck, her working as a party planner here didn't necessarily mean she was skilled. And Laney had told me they worked in teams, so she wasn't alone. All that said, though? Something smelled rotten, because *Allegra* wasn't even twenty yet. I knew that for sure.

"When did you last see her?" I asked. Because I hadn't been in the same room as Allegra since she'd been like twelve or thirteen.

"Couple years ago," Boone responded. "Her pop hired me to upgrade his wife's car with some security."

I raked my teeth over my lip, wondering how the fuck we were gonna get closer to Lange's files now. As part of the party planning crew, Allegra sat on valuable information. Whatever heist Darius was planning, I bet he'd want as many time frames as possible where he knew what was going on at another location. Allegra would know about the catering, about when meals would be served, everything from planned toasts to entertainment. In short, Allegra was key to pinning down a minute-by-minute schedule of Alfred Lange's whereabouts during the birthday shindig.

There was still the man in charge of the Langes' stay in general. We needed to get close to him too, because he would know even more. He'd have access to all reservations and when and where someone was being picked up by whatever car service they'd be using.

"I'll call TJ tomorrow," I said. "Whatever happens with Allegra, we're gonna need his approval."

Boone nodded firmly, then flicked a glance at something behind me. It was the bartender finishing up our drink order.

A thought struck me as I handed over a card to the bartender. "So that's why you were eye-fucking the girl? You recognized her."

Boone offered a confused expression before it morphed into amusement. "I wasn't eye-fucking her."

Sure, whatever. I'd said too much. I didn't want him to think I still got jealous. "Okay. Let's get back to the girls." After pocketing my card again, I grabbed three drinks and left two bottles for Boone to carry.

Goddammit. I had to be more subtle. I didn't want anything to get between us again, and that included my toxic possessiveness. I literally wanted to own the motherfucker. He was loved and adored by too many. I'd never suffered any shortage of friends—or hookups, for that matter—but Boone was definitely more lovable. He had a smile for everyone, whereas no matter how happy I was, I had a resting bitch face.

On our way back to our table, Boone stopped me in the middle of the crowd with a hand along my side. He got way too close, his chest against my back, and spoke in my ear again.

"I'm only gonna say this once." His voice and close proximity forced a shiver through me, and I swallowed the unease crawling up my throat. "You don't have anything to worry about. I'll never hurt you again."

Fuck me.

It was as reassuring as it was mortifying. I felt weak and pathetic. At the same time, I couldn't bring myself to joke it off, because I needed to cling to that promise more than I was willing to admit. Even if it meant he suspected that I still had all the wrong feelings for him.

"Let's focus on work," I replied, because I had to change the topic. "Whether or not we can use Allegra, we still need as many details as we can get our hands on."

I continued toward our table, unable to look back and read Boone's expression. It was too much.

Dinner revolved around only one thing—being nice and interesting enough that Laney and Allegra wanted to grab more drinks afterward. Boone and I were careful not to broach any topic that might link Allegra's background to ours, so we kept personal shit vague. Boone was a mechanic, which wasn't technically a lie; he just didn't work as one. And when Allegra asked what I did for a living, I said I was in between jobs.

It didn't feel awesome trying to get Allegra to reveal shit about her work, and not because of her family. Her ID might say she was in her twenties and named Alex, but we knew better. The girl was still a kid. She shouldn't be here.

After dinner, Boone excused himself to go meet up with Ma, and Ace wasn't too happy about leaving. She wanted to stay and work with her daddies, even though she had no idea what we were doing. It didn't seem to matter.

Laney excused herself too, to go to the bathroom.

I stuck my card into the leather binder the server had brought us, not even looking at the receipt. Wasn't my money.

I didn't know where we'd go from here. The casino downstairs would be too much of a distraction. It wasn't exactly a place to get someone drunk and extract information from them. Fuck—what would TJ say, huh?

So far, we hadn't learned much. We knew Allegra was actually in charge of the crew of three Venetian employees who would handle Lange's birthday party, and we'd learned her new "work project" was fun. That was all. Digging deeper, asking for details about the client, would look too suspicious.

"You don't recognize me, do you?" Allegra cocked her head at me, and she was grinning.

It made me narrow my eyes. Was she about to drop the act?

"What do you mean?" I played dumb and leaned back in my seat.

She bit her lip, calculating, without a hint of wariness in her eyes. "My real name isn't Alex."

Oh, she was actually...yeah, okay. Fuck pretending, then. "I know who you are."

She sat a little straighter and lifted a brow at me. "Why didn't you say something?"

Simple. "'Cause it's none of my business. This is your workplace. For all I know, you're up to something and need to stay under the radar." Man, I hoped that wasn't the case.

It was great to have TJ as a buddy, great to have him on my side, but that could change. You didn't wanna get too involved in anything that was their territory. It was why we had to tread really fucking carefully around Allegra.

"It's just a job," she replied with a slight shrug. "I want to show my parents I can manage on my own."

Hmm. This was more than a job, though. It was a position that required four years in college, for one.

"I think you're here on a job too," she stated and lifted her chin. The challenge in her eyes dared me to defy her. "The question is, how involved is Laney? Because she was very eager to bring me with her tonight, and she couldn't stop talking about you. You, specifically, as if she was trying to set us up. But the second I saw it was you..." She trailed off, not needing to spell out the obvious. She knew I was gay.

I couldn't help but smirk a little. I didn't see any reason to get worried or nervous, but I had to hand it to her. She was alert.

"It can't be about me," she went on. "You and your brother wouldn't do anything stupid."

Oh, we were plenty stupid, though she was right in this case. Allegra was protected. Hell, even by us. If she faced problems anywhere, Boone and I wouldn't hesitate to help, just like we could count on TJ and DJ to have our backs.

"At this point, it's better we go through your cousins," I told her. "We won't involve you."

That did something to her. It was as if she'd been struck—hard—and her eyes flashed with a plea. "You can't. TJ would pull the plug on me so fast. Please—can't we handle it between us? I'm at my wit's end here. If they start meddling again, I swear I'll leave the state."

I felt my eyebrows rise at the desperation in her tone. She wasn't kidding around. She didn't want her family involved one bit, which made me curious about her situation. How much did she think she was hiding from them? From my understanding, the women in their family had virtually no privacy, mainly because they kept their security tighter than a virgin asshole.

"You realize the guys have eyes and ears all over the Vegas, right?" I had to make sure she understood that. "If you haven't told them you work here, they've figured it out on their own."

"Of course they know," she responded in a rush. "It was DJ who helped me set up a new identity. But they gave me a warning—slightest indication of trouble and they'll tell my dad. And *he* doesn't know. Well, not the whole story. He knows I'm working."

Uh-huh. Even that was naïve. Her father was one of the

highest-ranking members of their organization. Trust, he knew everything.

"Look." She leaned forward, evidently ready to bargain. It was written all over her face. "If you're gonna go through my cousins to get something that you'd originally intended to get directly from me, it means it's something I can do. The way I see it, they don't have to know a damn thing. I know how to keep quiet. Do you?"

It wasn't a matter of being able to keep quiet. "I have a responsibility toward your cousins, Allegra. You gotta under-stand that."

"Which is always about my safety!" she pleaded imploringly. "I know you're obligated to tell them if you think I'm getting myself into trouble or whatever. But I'm not. I clearly have something you want—so it's up to you. Is this, whatever you want, gonna put me in harm's way?"

I frowned. "Of-fucking-course not."

"Then..." She gave me a look, at a loss, not seeing why we couldn't handle this between us. And I was starting to think she was making sense. "Let this be a simple exchange between you and me. You want something—I want something. As long as I don't risk anything, why go to my family?"

Back up. What did she want?

Unfortunately, we didn't get further than that because Laney returned, and it was fucking frustrating. I composed my face and did my best not to ask my friend to take a hike for five minutes. To be honest, if I could avoid involving TJ, that was the route I wanted to go down. I just had to make sure I could do it with a clean conscience.

"Did I miss anything fun?" Laney asked and plopped down in her seat.

Allegra sent me a flirtatious smile. "Actually, I'm really tired, so I was just about to ask Casey to walk me out."

I exhaled a chuckle and felt the frustration dissipate.

Laney looked like a combination of proud matchmaker and...well, she was a good person, so I could tell she felt a bit guilty too.

"Sure, I can walk you out." I pushed back my chair and stood up. "I'll be right back," I told Laney. Then I waited while the girls said their goodbyes before I ushered Allegra out of the dining room, then past the bar area too.

"I'm gonna give you the benefit of the doubt since you're TJ's friend," she said as we reached the indoor plaza. She peered up at me. "Here's what I want. There's a man working in Hospitality. His wife is cheating on him—relentlessly. And I wouldn't mind if he found out about that, preferably before he gives a certain job to his wife's obnoxious daughter."

Jesus Christ, she was well and truly a part of her family. I didn't know if Allegra had her eyes set on the job or the guy; it didn't matter. It was nothing I couldn't handle.

"That's it?" I asked. "You want pictures of his wife's affairs to show up on his desk or something?"

Allegra shifted her weight from one foot to the other and glanced around us, maybe making sure no one was listening. Cute. "That actually sounds perfect. Can you make that happen?"

Oh, I could. I chuckled. "Sure. Just give me his information."

Her brown eyes flashed with relief and a bit of excitement. "So what is it you want from me?"

Shit, we might actually pull this off without any hassle or risks. "Access to one of your clients' files."

She cocked her head, curious. "Whose? I only have two at the moment."

"Alfred Lange." I watched the recognition flick across her features. "All of it—whatever you're planning for his birthday party. Dates, reservations, specific times, guest totals, the whole thing."

She straightened and hiked her purse over her shoulder. "Would there be any risk of it tracing back to me?"

"None," I replied. "You just share whatever information you have with me—and keep me updated on changes." I'd make sure she knew where to be and not to be during the events too, but no need to scare her with that right now.

I kept my gaze locked with hers as I noticed Boone crossing the plaza behind Allegra.

"Okay. Deal." She extended her hand.

I smirked faintly and shook it. "Perfect. Clear your schedule after work tomorrow. We'll meet up and discuss details."

"Got it. Um, should we exchange numbers?"

I shook my head. "Won't be necessary. When do you get off work? I'll get you a new phone you can contact me on." With her background, she was probably not a stranger to throwaways.

"I have a wedding next weekend, so I start working double shifts tomorrow," she said. "But I have a three-hour break at four."

"That works," I replied with a nod. "Let's meet up outside Taco Bell at four thirty, then. The one that serves booze."

She snickered. "I'll be there. This will be fun!"

I let out a chuckle and shook my head. "The apple doesn't fall far."

She smirked at that.

EIGHT

"What do you think, Daddy?"

I looked away from my magazine and stared at my nails. "They've never looked so good, princess." Who knew purple was my color? "Maybe you can do nails when you grow up."

She beamed and tucked away her nail polishes into her toiletry bag. "When's Dad coming?"

Soon. Too soon. I checked the clock over the TV and sighed to myself. "Twenty minutes." Which meant I had to get out of here.

I wasn't sure I could do this much longer. It'd been almost four years, and my own brother still couldn't face me unless he had to.

Every week when Ace's pickup time rolled around, I was dragged further down into a pit of despair.

Wasn't the pain supposed to fade over time?

———

By the time Boone and I were walking away from the plaza and all the restaurants, I could tell I needed to clue my brother in before he lost it.

"Mind telling me why we just said goodbye to Laney and the mafia princess?" he asked, frustrated. "We're supposed to be heading to a bar with them now."

"I already took care of shit," I answered. "It's practically in the bag. I'll explain when we get upstairs."

I guessed we didn't need Ma to babysit Ace after all.

"Wait." Boone grabbed my shoulder and halted our step. "You're saying everything's taken care of? We'll have the info we need?"

"Yeah. Tomorrow—Allegra and I struck a deal."

Boone was itching to hear the details, but it seemed he had something else on his agenda first. "Then why go upstairs? We have—" he checked his watch "—five hours until Mom's going back home."

My gaze got caught on the pizza slice pin on his shirt, and it made me look down at the pin Ace had given me. Heading upstairs and letting Mom go home early meant we might get another family moment like before—and I craved them like heroin—but on the other hand...

"What do you have in mind?" I asked him.

He grinned. "A fucking bar, obviously. We haven't gone out together, just you and me, in four years."

His grin was infectious, and there was no need to twist my arm. I was game.

Twenty minutes later, we stepped out of a cab outside Mandalay Bay and made our way into the casino. Of all the bars in Vegas, EyeCandy was in my top three, no doubt. It had a sweet vibe with its interactive dance floor and cozy booths, and nothing catapulted me back to the eighties and nineties like leather furniture lit up in purple and a DJ playing Cher.

It was one of my favorite remixes, to boot.

Maybe I would've gone with another song, but the DJ couldn't know that I'd had "Strong Enough" on an endless loop for a month after shoving Boone out of my life.

"This goddess helped me get past our breakup," I half joked and slapped Boone on the back. "Don't read into the lyrics, 'cause they're entirely too accurate."

Why did I have to be so goddamn honest all of a sudden?

I blew out a breath and aimed for the bar. I was in a Gimlet mood.

The place was barely half full, and it felt too intimate to grab a booth, so I parked my ass on one of the stools at the bar and gave the bartender a chin-nod. Boone got settled next to me and spun his stool to face the dance floor.

"What do you want?" I asked him.

He squinted at the bar over his shoulder. "Uhh... Negroni."

Nasty. I couldn't stomach Campari since we'd stolen a bottle from Ma in high school.

"Do you remember...?"

He let out a chuckle and spun around in his seat again. "I thought we were gonna have to take you to the hospital."

I shuddered.

After ordering our drinks and opening a tab, I glanced behind me, surveying the crowd tonight, and bobbed my head absently to the new pop remix playing.

I was gonna feel more upbeat soon, right? It felt forced now.

"What did we get wasted on after we learned we were gonna be Ace's guardians?"

I hummed and thought back. That'd been some cheap, foul shit too. "Some peach liqueur. Christ, Ma has shitty taste in booze."

Boone grinned but said nothing.

Maybe he was thinking on those days too. We'd been terrified. A single phone call was all it'd taken. We'd gone from believing that grieving a lost friend was the worst that could happen, to discovering there was a toddler out there with our name on her. And then when the lawyer asked if we would proceed with Tia's wishes and actually take care of this slip of a girl... I shook my head to myself. We'd been two dumbasses; of course we'd hesitated first. Even as we knew there'd been no option. If our friend's final wish was for us to raise her daughter, so be it.

Boone nudged my shoulder with his. "What would we do without her today, huh?"

I didn't wanna think about it. As soon as the bartender handed us our drinks, I held up my glass. "To the best daughter in the universe."

He clinked his glass to mine and took a swig.

I followed suit and felt the lime and the gin explode in my mouth.

Back in the day, I didn't need a drink to get me in a party mood. Now, I was waiting for the alcohol to make me feel similar urges as in the past, to hit up a club, to go crazy, to sneak in to pool parties, to drive out into the desert and run around just for stupid kicks that only made sense after a line of blow.

Growing up, I'd just never had any fear. I'd thrown myself into the dumbest dares and most reckless ruses, knowing I'd be okay in the end because Boone had always been next to me. We'd protected each other.

"Why are you lookin' all broody?" he asked.

I smiled ruefully and emptied my drink, then gestured to the bartender for a new round of the same. "I'm getting old and nostalgic."

He smiled back. "Bring me with you."

I chuckled and ran a hand through my hair. "How many pool parties and nightclubs have we snuck in to over the years?"

"Hundreds. It's the duty of a Vegas kid."

I exhaled a laugh.

"Yeah, maybe. I'm not really feeling it anymore, though." I dropped my chin in my hand and rested my elbow on the bartop. "I want barbecues and soccer games and watching Ace light up at a new pin."

Boone nodded and dropped his gaze to his drink, though not before I got a glimpse of the same desire in his eyes. Maybe that was why he was pushing for a house. He wanted to settle down and have family moments too.

Jesus Christ, how I'd missed having him in my life. The fucker gave my life meaning. Without him and our girl... Another thing I didn't wanna think about. It physically hurt.

"I know the feeling," he said into his glass. At the same time, my second drink arrived. "I think there's still some hell-raisin' left in us, though. Hey," he addressed the bartender. "You got bottle service around here?"

I cocked a brow at him.

"Yes, sir." The bartender reached for something under the bar and produced a tablet. "Our menu is right here." The screen came to life and showed items only idiots would pay that much money for. For chrissakes, I didn't even wanna use someone else's credit card for a $500 bottle of vodka.

Soon as the bartender gave us some space, I leaned in and eyed the menu closer. "Are you outta your damn mind?"

"Oh, come on." Solid argument by my brother. "I have no interest in setting you loose in a club, but I'm not ready to head back to the hotel room. I want drinks and a trip down memory lane. Does that work, princess?"

I tapped my fingers over my lips and couldn't help but grin. It was what he did to me. Same thing back at the Venetian when he'd suggested we go to a bar. His mood was contagious.

"It works for me," I said.

"Good. Now, help me pick an outrageously marked-up package deal."

Deal implied bargain; this was the opposite. Thankfully, we weren't the ones getting robbed.

I took a swig of my gimlet and peered at the offers that included gin. One package stood out. A small bottle of vodka, a small bottle of gin, six beers, six hard lemonades, and mixers. Oh, you got snacks too. I was a big fan.

"That one." I pointed to it.

Boone approved and flagged down the bartender again.

So that was how we ended up in one of the smaller, circular booths a little while later. The backs of the booths were high, and as if that didn't provide enough seclusion, they were draped too, leaving only the entrance open. And we had our selection of drinks on ice on our table, including a tray with lime wedges, orange slices, and lemon rinds. Fancy shit.

While I dragged a couple nachos through the guac, Boone decided to mix us two gin and tonics.

This was better. More comfortable. Much less noisy.

Over the next drink and two beers, I explained what Allegra and I had agreed to, after which Boone and I discussed our immediate plans. I knew he wanted to take that trip down memory lane, but we had work to cover too. I wanted to get that out of the way, including how we divvied up the workload.

We decided that Boone would take over for me and keep an eye on AJ Lange's habits, while I focused on Allegra's request to pin the cheating wife, because I assumed that would take a few days at least. Possibly more. I could easily bring Ace with me too.

"Speaking of," he said. "I don't wanna do every other week with Ace anymore. I fucking hate it. I wanna be able to see her whenever."

I furrowed my brow and dumped a few ice cubes into my glass, then reached for the vodka. "What choice do we have?"

"That's a dumb question coming from the family's self-appointed brain and beauty," he replied. I laughed, couldn't help it. The drinks had warmed me up and loosened my tongue. "You can stop pushing me away and let me stay with you until we find a house."

Until *we*...

He narrowed his eyes at me—or tried. The booze had reached his head. His cheeks were a little flushed, and his blue eyes were slightly glazed over. "You're hesitatin'," he accused. "Why don't you wanna live with me? You said it yourself, we're the best family. And like the good old days—you're in charge of food and laundry. I tidy up and clean."

Fuckin' hell, he was going way too fast. "They're good old days to *you*, Boone. To me, it was..." Sheer agony. The best and the worst of all of it. Being so close to everything I wanted without actually having it.

I shook my head and emptied half a bottle of ginger ale into my vodka. Some lime followed in my lame attempt to create a Moscow mule without the proper ingredients.

"I thought we were gonna go slow." I took a long swig of my

drink, thankful that I didn't feel bad or anything. The topic would've been much more uncomfortable if I'd been sober.

"Slow sucks! Slow is keeping us apart."

I grinned lazily at his outburst. It was funny how the same words could have different meanings depending who spoke them. He was all about getting our family back together. If I'd uttered the words, "I don't want us to be apart," it would mean something else.

"I forgot what a whiny crybaby you can be," I drawled. "God forbid I leave my dirty clothes in the bathroom after I shower."

"Because they go in the fucking hamper two feet away," he snapped. "And you're one to talk. I accidentally put one of your CDs in the wrong case *once*, and ever since, I'm not allowed to go near your stereo."

"That's how CDs get lost forever!" All it took was one time.

The fucker flashed a grin at me. "See how good we are together? I make sure you put your dirty clothes away, and you keep me in line so no shitty '90s music disappears."

Okay, no need to trash-talk my favorite music.

"I'm not sure bickering like an old married couple qualifies as good together," I muttered into my drink.

Damn. I knew I was getting drunk when I barely tasted the vodka, and I hadn't skimped on it.

"You know I'm not gonna tell you no, Boone," I said, downing my drink. "All I'm asking is that we take our time."

"We will," he promised. "It'll be a while before we can afford a house anyway. That's why I think you should open your heart and let me stay with you. It'll give us a chance to get used to living together again."

I groaned through a laugh that felt full of hopelessness. He didn't get it. By going slowly, I meant I needed *space*. He couldn't be around me twenty-four seven. I'd lose my shit. Hell,

I'd already lost it. I was screwed. Completely. I'd known for years that there would be no getting over him, so while "taking it slow" was nothing but a feeble attempt at delaying the inevitable, it was all I had. I wasn't ready to become a basket case yet.

"Hey." He shifted in his seat to face me better, and he cupped the back of my neck. "Instead of focusing on what we might fuck up, let's talk about shit we're looking forward to. Such as throwing Ace a kick-ass birthday party in a few months where her dads aren't avoiding each other."

I chuckled and sucked some lime juice off the edge of my thumb.

"Maybe we could go somewhere?" he suggested.

I'd like that. "Sounds good. Just the three of us."

He smiled and let his hand drop, though he stayed close and dropped his forearms on the table. "Mexico will be nice that time of year."

It was insane how easily he opened up our future with those words. I could suddenly see all kinds of shit. Vacations, recitals that were about going together instead of just showing up in the same place to watch our daughter, holidays, not having to split a day into two, movie nights, heading over to Ma's as a family for Sunday dinner...

Mexico was a great idea. "I can think of worse ways to spend a couple weeks than lying on a beach and sipping cock-tails." Plus, Boone in board shorts was fucking pornographic. He got a nice tan too, and his dark hair became bleached as soon as he was near the ocean. "We'll probably need to throw Ace a children's party too, though. She'll want her friends to come over. Ma's place is better for that."

Last year, we'd put together a barbecue for Ace and five of her friends, but it'd been a little too cold for the kids. We'd need a better plan this year.

"Or we could turn your living room into a home theater," Boone suggested. "We'll need to be indoors, yeah? All we need is a big flat-screen or a projector—and a bunch of takeout and snacks."

Huh. Not a bad idea at all. "You're not as dumb as you look, big brother."

"Fuck you." He took a beer for himself. "You may see me as some worker bee who will only burn the midnight owl when I have clear instructions to follow, but I'm fucking intelligent."

I cocked my head and smiled, confused. "The midnight what?"

"What?" He scowled. "You heard me."

I smirked and told myself not to laugh, but Jesus fucking Christ—oh, I couldn't. One laugh slipped out, then another and another. Before I knew it, I was fucking howling. The midnight owl— "Ha!" I guffawed. Tears sprang to my eyes, and I clutched my stomach.

"Shut up!" he growled and shoved at me.

"Oh God," I wheezed through the laughter. "Oh, Boone. It's —It's..." I giggled like a fucking schoolgirl and wiped at my eyes. "You burn the midnight *oil*."

"What—no, fuck that. How does that make sense? Owls are night creatures. Nocturnal—that's the word. They're nocturnal!"

I cracked up all over again, and I gripped his bicep before he could take a swing at me, 'cause I knew that was coming up next if I didn't calm the hell down soon.

"Are you done?" he griped.

"Almost," I laughed, dropping my forehead to his shoulder. "I'm trying—don't hit me."

He scoffed. "Don't hit me," he mocked in a child's voice. "Ace told me you've been bragging about your new muscles. I don't see 'em."

That worked. Some annoyance mingled with the amusement, and I lifted my head to glare at him. Only, I couldn't fucking hold it. I was in too high spirits.

I ended up smiling instead. "Hey, my abs show now, and look—" I flexed my bicep for him.

It bulged like a motherfucker through my shirt, causing the fabric to stretch.

Boone wasn't impressed. "Cute."

It was no use. I huffed and poured another drink instead. We couldn't all burn the midnight owl to look like monster beefcakes.

I snorted a laugh to myself and went bottoms up with my screwdriver. Important to get my shot of vitamin C for the day.

"I'm really glad we came out." I stifled a belch into my fist. "Oh fuck—this song!" It was as if I'd forgotten there was music at all—until the right tune penetrated the bubble I was in. And the right song would always be "Be My Lover" by La Bouche. It woke me the fuck up, and I started moving to the beat. This was *gold.*

Boone merely stared at me, amusement tugging at his lips.

I didn't feel old anymore. I felt...hungry. Invigorated. I couldn't sit still any longer.

"It's always the same with you," he chuckled. "Like a flip of a switch—every single time."

"Whattaya mean?" I peered closer at him. "I don't know what you mean, but I reject what you're saying."

He laughed. "I just mean, maybe you require more drinks now to get in the mood, but something always sets you off once you're out." He paused. "I can't tell you how many times you pissed me off way back when, when I wanted to drag you out and you didn't feel like it. 'Cause I knew you'd like it once you got going."

Oh—because he didn't know that I was full of it. "I lied to

you back then." I waved him off. Clearly he was wrong, because he didn't have the whole picture. "I usually wanted to go out, but I didn't wanna see a bunch of women draped over you, so..." I shrugged.

Was that too honest? I couldn't be sure anymore.

I scratched my neck and squinted at Boone, finding him smirking at me.

Fucker.

I'd been too honest.

He tilted his head at me, observing me, which wasn't his style—he wasn't an observer—and had an annoying little smile playing on his lips. "You wanna hit up a club now? I can get us into Hakkasan if you want."

I bet he could. He used to work as a bouncer there, when we weren't on speaking terms.

"How much time do we got left?" I asked.

He checked his watch. "Three hours and change."

I glanced out at the dance floor. Compared to the ones at Hakkasan, it was pathetic. But this wasn't a club. It was a bar with a dance floor. Hakkasan, on the other hand, was huge. Five stories. They went all out with light shows and the best DJs in the world.

"I don't know if it matters these days," Boone said, side-eyeing me, "but there won't be any women draped over me."

Shit. I swallowed hard and quickly poured a double shot of vodka into my glass. Then I squeezed some lime in there before I threw it back. There wasn't a chance in hell I was going to answer him. Fuck that. He knew too much already.

"It matters. Let's go." There was something wrong with me. I'd *just* decided not to tell him more, goddammit. Only one way to get out of this sticky mess, and it was to drink myself into oblivion.

"Good." He threw back a shot too, and I narrowed my eyes

at him. But I forgot why. What was *good*? That we were heading to a club? Yeah, I agreed. I needed to shake what my mama had given me.

Unfortunately, going to a house club meant there wouldn't be a whole lot of shaking going on. After closing our tab and taking a cab over to Hakkasan, we got treated like sexy women. Aka, no line, no entry fee. We went straight through, and Boone fist-bumped his buddies at the entrance. We made it past the bars and went to the main club area where a sea of people were jumping up and down to the deafening music. Modern music. House music that shot its heartbeat through us along with a bolt of adrenaline.

A sped-up version of Tiësto's "Red Lights" pumped through the massive club, accompanied by a light show that matched the beat and the title of the song.

Even though it wasn't my favorite genre, it kinda took my breath away and sucked me in. Without glancing behind me, without making sure Boone was with me, I surrendered to the pull and lost myself in the crowd.

Holy shit, it'd been too long since I'd done this. It was liberating. Maybe Boone was right. Maybe I still had some hell-raisin' in me. Red lights traveled across the floor, and smoke billowed out next, followed by red lasers and a bright static that made everything look like life was shot in slow motion.

The only thing missing now was a pair of strong hands on me, but we couldn't get everything we wanted.

I closed my eyes instead, as the song started morphing into something very familiar, and it plastered a wide smile on my face. *Fuck. Yes.* Darude, "Sandstorm." Now, this shit brought me back. It was nothing short of electrifying. The people around me went wild, and the lights changed to blue and neon green. My heart pounded faster than I could jump, sweat beaded across my body, my breaths came out shallow, and my mind swam in flashing colors and alcohol.

I lost track of time and space. The music owned my body, and Boone owned the rest. I didn't know where he was, but I knew he was close. I felt it in my gut. Knowing him, he'd bought a drink or something. He wasn't one to lose it on the dance floor.

Thinking about him made my heart squeeze. I'd gone too long without checking in with him, and the new song sealed the deal. An Avicii track. The lyrics told me to live a life that I would remember, to have nights that would never die, and it punched an urgency into me. I swallowed dryly and stopped moving. Everyone around me did the opposite. It was a calmer song compared to the rest, one actually worth dancing to, and I stared blearily at the excitement I was surrounded by.

Then my gaze landed on an unmoving figure. Boone. Spotlights in reds, yellows, and oranges blazed a trail of fire through the crowd, and he was the only one standing still. Watching me.

I smiled, feeling weirdly unsure. I had a knot in my stomach that alcohol usually took care of. It was supposed to.

I maneuvered my way past a group of dancers and their flailing limbs, which were more like weapons, and dodged a couple elbows before I reached him.

I didn't even try to say something. I could barely hear my own thoughts.

Boone stuck an empty beer bottle into his pocket, then closed the distance between us by gripping my belt. I grinned, wondering if he was actually gonna attempt a conversation here. Spoiler alert, it wouldn't work. But that didn't stop him from cupping the back of my neck and dipping down to press his forehead to mine. Seriously, I wouldn't hear a word— Except, he had no intention of saying anything. He kissed me. His warm lips touched mine softly, one brush, two.

I reeled back as the shock hit me with a sharp twinge, and I frowned. What was he— Fuck. He couldn't fucking do that to me.

The alcohol made me see things that weren't there. There was no way he was staring at me with desire. The hesitation in his eyes made sense, not the rest. But when he tried again, all my defenses shut down. He kissed me harder and moved his hands to frame my jaw, to keep me in place.

Don't hurt me. Asshole.

A sluggish stream of lust started coursing through my system. I collapsed like a house of cards, and I screwed my eyes shut. This was gonna kill me tomorrow, wasn't it? Not that it stopped me from kissing him back. Even as I kept my hands against my sides, balled into fists, I couldn't resist kissing him. Oh, fuck me sideways, the lust took over and heated me up, and before I knew it, my traitorous hands were sliding up his chest.

I sucked in a breath and locked my arms around his neck, and he pulled me even closer with a hand on my back. We deepened the kiss at the same time, and when our tongues met, I went off the deep end. There would be no going back. Ever.

Bizarre, absurd, crazy, surreal, *unreal*, no word was good enough to describe how well and truly he'd fucked up my head now, to stand here in the middle of a nightclub with people bumping into us while I made out with *him*. My everything.

My lungs burned, and all I did was go deeper. I pushed my tongue into his mouth and kissed him hungrily, desperately, figuring I might as well take as much as I could. Enjoy the ride. Make the night last. Right? The song had told me to chase unforgettable nights.

He gave me an overwhelming, passionate, drugging kiss that cracked my chest wide open, before he started slowing us down. And I felt robbed. Already an addict.

With the last brushing kiss, I forced my eyes open again and found his heavy gaze piercing me. If this was how it was gonna be, he could hurt me forever. I was powerless.

He jerked his chin toward the exit, and I nodded dumbly.

I followed him as the knot in my stomach both grew tighter and doubled in size.

Was I gonna have to remind my brother that he was into women?

Seemed like something people would remember, their own sexuality.

The summer heat outside offered no relief whatsoever, and I could feel my drunkenness shifting over to the part of the night when it was time to wind down. If I drank any more now, I'd just get sick. Maybe I still would. I was starting to get woozy.

I needed to take a leak too. It was a wonder we hadn't broken the seal yet.

Boone kept walking until we were almost back to the start of the Strip, near the Hershey store. On the last stretch of the side street that was somewhat quiet, he stopped and faced me.

"Can you trust me enough not to ask any questions about this?" he asked.

Uh. "You expect me to let—"

"Yeah." He took a step closer to me. "I need you to trust me to not hurt you again, but I'm not ready to talk. All I know is that if you walk outta my life again, I'll be done for. I gotta have you close—ridiculously close, evidently."

Ridiculously close.

Kinda hard not to feel reassured by that, despite that it didn't tell me what he actually meant. I folded my arms over my chest, a weak attempt to protect myself, maybe, and I stared at the ground, trying to get my brain to function.

"I know I'm asking a lot, Case."

I snorted softly. *I'll say.* He could push me to invite him to live with me, he could drag painful confessions out of me, apparently he could kiss me too, but I wasn't allowed to ask anything in return?

Perhaps it didn't matter. I'd already admitted to myself that I didn't stand a chance against him.

He came even closer, and it made me hyperaware of his proximity. When less than a foot separated us, I stiffened as he grazed his lips along my jaw. Part of me couldn't believe it was happening. After so many years of hating my own feelings, of fantasizing about what it would be like to feel his beard tickling my neck, of wondering how it'd be to make out with him, suck his cock, fuck him, get railed by him—shit. I had to stop those thoughts.

"You make me lose my goddamn mind," he murmured.

I drew an unsteady breath and tilted my face toward his. "Yeah, feeling's mutual, buddy."

He smirked faintly right before he captured my mouth in a kiss. It melted me in a second and shot desire down my body, but the pleasure was short-lived. The second I closed my eyes, I was overcome by a dizzy spell, and I clutched his arms.

"Shit." I broke the kiss and swallowed hard.

"You okay?" He looked worried—and a little amused. "I forget you can't handle your liquor like me."

"Fuck you." I stepped away from his personal space and leaned against the wall instead. "You're a three-hundred-pound sponge."

He let out a laugh and retrieved his phone. "Two seventy-five, actually. I'm getting us an Uber. You need food and a bed."

Nope, nope, nope, I needed to barf. I pressed a fist to my mouth as nausea rushed up my throat.

NINE

He offered a hand.

I took his arm.

I couldn't help it. Being welcomed back into his life gave me a reason to wake up in the morning. I clung to every word he said and watched his lips as he spoke. I registered his body language and every gesture, forcing me to pay attention to his physical appearance. The need kept growing stronger, and my obsession wasn't going anywhere. I catalogued every feature. His trimmed beard, his intense eyes, the jokes and filth that came from his lips, his arms and thighs, his abs, his runner's body and sleek muscles, his wolfish smirks and slanted grins.

I was losing it. Fast.

What the fuck was happening to me?

"Shh! Be quiet. I don't want Ace to wake up." I took a huge bite of my sandwich and leaned against the wall next to the door.

Boone shook his head and pulled out his keycard. "Then quit yelling."

I wasn't yelling. He was yelling.

With the door open, I stumbled inside and kicked off my shoes. The bathroom was right there—it had my name on it. I was as hungry as I was nauseated, so I figured I'd go in there and eat and puke. Rinse and repeat. Then shower. Man, I wanted a shower.

Ma appeared in the hallway, and I smiled widely and went over to hug her.

"Hey, Mom. How you doin'? Have I told you lately how much I love you?"

"Oh, for Pete's sake. How much have you had to drink, sugar?"

"Two beers!" I let her go and took another bite from my sandwich. It was really good. Boone had picked it up for me while I'd waited in the Uber. Like a patty melt but on a baguette and with garlic butter and pickles. "By the way, some asshole threw up in the elevator."

Mom shot me a look before she gave Boone a similar one, but with more annoyance. "What's wrong with you? You know your brother can't drink as much as you can. It's your responsibility to look out for him."

She was so right! I waved my sandwich at her. "Yeah, what she said."

Boone turned incredulous. "What the hell? Last time I checked, he was a grown man."

I shrugged and chewed on a mouthful of delicious food. "Admit it, you just wanted to drink me under the table so you could take advantage." Ignoring Boone's warning glare, I faced Mom again. "He put his tongue in my mouth, Mom."

Mom raised her brows and eyed us both. Then she shook her head and disappeared into the suite, only to return a few seconds later with her purse. "I don't know what the fuck you're on, but you make sure to sober up, stat. You hear me, boys? We'll talk tomorrow."

She patted our cheeks before walking out, and I had to be real quick before I lost her.

"But, *Mom.*" I stuck my head out the door. "You didn't tell me you love me back."

She sighed and offered an indulgent smile. "I love you both to stupid measures. Now, please, for the love of God, do not wake up Paisley."

I grinned. "We won't. Did y'all have a nice time?"

"We always do, sugar. Go back inside and get some rest."

"Yes, ma'am."

I brought my sandwich into the bathroom and sat down on the edge of the tub. I'd plant my merry ass on the shitter if it weren't in its own little space, and I'd just get lonely in there. I wanted company. To be honest, I hadn't felt sick in probably over five minutes, so maybe I was done throwing up. That would be great. It meant I'd be better company to Boone too, who came in with a change of clothes for me. Or a pair of boxer shorts and a tee anyway.

"I'm thirsty," I informed him.

"You're chatty as fuck too." He placed my clothes between the two sinks. "I'll be right back. Don't do anything stupid."

"Like what?" I polished off the rest of my sandwich and

threw the wrapper in the bathtub. I wasn't supposed to throw shit on the floor.

Boone snorted on his way out. "I ain't giving you ideas."

I didn't need ideas. I needed to strip. I couldn't shower with clothes on. As I stood up and started removing my belt, I caught sight of our toiletries on the sink, and I had to smile. Ma had placed my toothbrush next to one sink and Boone's next to the other, and Ace's was in between the two. But if he moved in with us, we'd share a sink, and it definitely wouldn't be made out of marble.

Boone returned by the time I was throwing my shirt over the chair by the vanity, and he had a Coke and a bottle of water for me.

He looked a little put off. I didn't like that.

"Are you mad at me?" I asked.

He pulled out a bottle of painkillers from his pocket and shot me a wry smirk. "I wouldn't say mad."

"What would you say, then?" I pushed down my pants and underwear, then removed my socks too.

Boone averted his gaze and leaned against the sink. "Frustrated. All kinds of frustrated."

"Oh." I didn't know what to say to that. Instead, I downed two painkillers with a couple mouthfuls of water. Room-temperature water. Fuck that. I opened the Coke next. It was ice-cold.

Goddamn, that felt good.

After draining half the bottle, I picked up my toothbrush and noticed Boone staring at me and trying to be discreet about it. More accurately, he was checking out my stomach. Yeah, I bet he hadn't believed me when I'd told him my abs showed a little now. That'd show the fucker! I hadn't been lying.

"When did you do this one?" He brushed his fingers over a tattoo along my rib cage. It was my latest piece, a heavily shadowed image of Boone's first car. A blue, American classic that we used to drive out into the desert to get high in.

"Last year, I think." I squeezed some toothpaste onto my toothbrush, then headed for the shower next to the bathtub. I wanted to get more ink, but I was running out of places to put it. Boone had more space on his torso. Mostly his back and his shoulders were tatted up—and one that snaked down from his shoulder to the side of his ribs. But his chest was free of ink, unlike mine. And I hoped it stayed that way, 'cause his chest was magnificent as it was. Plus, he had more chest hair than me, and that was just sexy as shit.

Talk about luxury, the water turned hot right away. I stepped under the spray and began brushing my teeth, and I contemplated asking why he was still here. Although I was far from sober, I didn't feel sick anymore, and the earth wasn't spinning as quickly either. In half an hour or so, I'd even be able to close my eyes without getting dizzy.

"Boone?"

"Yeah?"

"Are you enjoying the show?"

He sighed heavily and didn't say anything.

I grinned to myself and spat out some toothpaste. Shame I couldn't see his facial features properly through the glass.

I bet I was hot when I gargled.

He'd kissed me tonight. That was wild. It'd actually happened.

I twisted my body and cupped my hand under the body wash dispenser. "Are you pissed I told Ma you had your wicked way with me?"

Boone left the sink and sat down at the vanity instead, so I guess he wasn't leaving anytime soon.

"Not really." He yawned. "I know your mouth runs when you're drunk."

Hey. I was offended. The truth was, it depended on the topic. I'd never compromise any work shit or say anything Ace shouldn't hear.

"My mouth can do a lot of things," I chose to say instead.

He didn't reply now either. Bastard.

I let it go and focused on soaping up. The hot water was quickly draining me of my last energy, and I was looking forward to falling asleep. Boone could take the bed with Ace. I'd been told I snored like a motherfucker after a night out. Besides, the sectional in the sitting area looked plenty comfy.

"I'll sleep on the couch, by the way." I tilted my head back and let the water wash me clean. No dizziness when I closed my eyes—score.

"All right. I'll, uh...I'll go prepare it for you."

I cracked one eye open and watched him walk out. There wasn't much to prepare. We'd been given spare sheets and whatever for Ace; I could grab that myself.

When I was done, I stepped out of the shower and wrapped a towel around my hips.

My reflection in the mirror made me wince, so I didn't linger. I dried off hurriedly before I put on my boxer briefs, and then I took myself and my bloodshot eyes outta the bathroom.

I paused at the bed, seeing Ace's hair splayed all over her pillow, and I couldn't keep myself from walking over to her side. It was a magnetic pull that I had no control over. She was asleep and hugging a stuffed animal to her—a birthday present from Boone, if I wasn't mistaken. I bent down and brushed a kiss to her forehead, and I fucking hated how quickly she was growing up. From the age of four, she'd been a tiny adult. It wasn't often she slept with her stuffies anymore.

"Case."

I straightened and glanced over at Boone. Maybe he was worried I was gonna wake her up. The couch was visible through the railing dividing the suite, and he'd prepared one side of the couch for me. The only thing that stood between me and crisp sheets now was Boone himself. There were two steps, and I could only descend one of them because he was blocking the way.

I lifted a brow in question, even though he wasn't making eye contact. His tired gaze roamed my body instead, and his inner turmoil suddenly became painfully clear to me. He couldn't make heads or tails of what he was feeling.

"I don't know what to do when close isn't close enough." His low, rough voice shook me with the openhearted plea in it.

"No, I think you know," I murmured. He was just afraid, and I got it. A lot was at stake. "But whatever you're going through, I'm here." It was terrifying to me too, but there was no alternative. I'd wanted him for so fucking long that even if this turned out to be a temporary phase of confusion for him, it didn't matter. He could use me. I had no pride or dignity in the matter.

I had very little hope, too, to be honest. Boone had always been straighter than an arrow, and I was willing to bet he was mixing up his grief—missing me, wanting to raise Ace with me, be a family—with the types of feelings he otherwise reserved for women. But now I was back in his life, and perhaps he didn't know what to make of it.

"What do you wanna do right now?" I asked quietly.

He finally looked me in the eye, and there was no doubt about what he wanted. The fire ignited instantly. He closed the distance between us and kissed me, and I was fully prepared for once. I cupped his cheeks and pressed myself to him, feeling less cautious and a lot more demanding.

He was getting bolder too, and I fucking loved it. As I deepened the kiss, he slipped his hands underneath my boxer briefs and palmed my ass roughly, squeezing me to him. It shot a bolt of lust through me, and I moved my hands to the back of his head and my fingers into his hair.

He exhaled the sexiest groan when I tugged at his hair, so I made sure to do it again.

Despite that he only had a couple inches on me in height, it felt good to stand on the middle step and tower over him a little. It felt even better how he seemingly went all in and took everything I gave him. I wanted to go so much further, but I had to slow my roll.

I swept my tongue around his and tried to go for a more unhurried kiss. Not just for him, for me too. If I kept going much longer, I'd be hard as a rock.

I didn't wanna stop kissing him, though. His lips felt too fucking good against my own. Warm, both soft and firm, with the sexy rasp of our beards.

"Go take a shower." I had to clear the lust out of my voice. I wasn't sure what turned me on the most, kissing him or feeling his cock getting hard against my thigh. "When you're done, go to bed if you're tired. Or—come to me, and I'll take care of you."

He shuddered and inched back a little. "Don't put those thoughts in my head."

I mustered a ghost of a smile and kissed him quickly. "I'm not asking for anything in return, and I won't push you. But I won't lie. I want that cock in my throat."

"Jesus." He took another step back and scrubbed his hands over his face. "The thoughts are in my head now, jackass."

I chuckled and passed him on the way to the couch.

I was passed out seconds after my head hit the pillow, so it was totally up to him what happened next. Either he woke me up and got head, or we'd wake up at the same time when Ace deemed it was time to get breakfast.

Neither happened. As if my body had been expecting it, I went from fast asleep to wide awake when Boone crawled under the duvet with me sometime later. He couldn't have come straight from his shower. For one, his hair was dry. For two, the night sky was giving way to a new day, slowly but surely.

We had maybe an hour or two before Ace would be up.

"What time is it?" I whispered.

"Five." He pulled the duvet higher up and landed on the pillow. "I just wanna be close to you."

I swallowed past the dryness in my throat and shifted an arm under his head. "Okay. I'm right here." He looked like he hadn't slept much. I was ready to get a few more Z's, though. I didn't wanna move around too much either, 'cause I could sense a headache threatening to overtake if I got cocky.

He sighed contentedly and buried his face against my neck, and I wrapped my arms around him and welcomed one of his legs between mine.

"So you robbed me of getting you off, huh?"

"Yeah. Sorry. Jacked it in the shower."

"Hmpf."

I felt his sleepy smile against my skin, and I kissed him on the forehead.

"Aren't you gonna ask me what got me off?" he asked quietly.

Maybe I should since he'd brought it up.

"Tell me."

He hummed and stretched out alongside me. "Your, uh, fingers in my ass."

"Fuck me," I mouthed into the darkness. Then I turned onto my side, wanting to get closer. "Yeah, whenever you wanna explore that, you lemme know."

He chuckled with a pinch of nervousness in his voice, and that was so unlike Boone. He didn't do nervous.

"My big bear." I threw caution to the wind and reached down to grope his ass. Fuck, how he turned me on. He was big all over. And now it was difficult to sleep. I couldn't even keep my head on the pillow. I had to look at him. For every minute that went by, the sky outside provided more light so I could see him clearer. "You're so fucking hot."

He let out a breath and ended up on his back. "Don't turn me on again. I just wanna hold you."

Always the sweetheart.

"Give me two minutes with your chest." I didn't wait for his response. I dipped down and nuzzled his pec, feeling his chest hair tickle my lips. Until I reached a nipple.

He shivered when I closed my mouth around it. His fingers disappeared into my hair next, and I was ready for him to pull me back at any moment. But before he did, I was gonna get my fill.

I touched him greedily, every inch that I'd only been allowed to stare at in secret. I kissed him too. Sucked on his flesh, nipped at him, and went a little crazy. Every time he tensed up, I felt his muscles underneath my fingers. A silent reminder that a steely beast rested under the soft teddy bear.

"Christ," he breathed.

It was tempting to try to seduce him. It would be so easy... While I kissed my way down to his stomach, it was impossible to miss his cock starting to strain in his boxers. The sight of him made my mouth water.

I reluctantly shifted upward again, leaving a trail of open-mouthed kisses until I got to his lips, and then he took over. He rolled half on top of me and kissed me hungrily, and he was quick to pull up the duvet once more. It was as if he were trying to keep us hidden in a cocoon.

"You weren't supposed to turn me on," he murmured in a gravelly tone.

I smiled against his lips. "My bad."

He let out a humming sound and squeezed me to him. "Right now, everything is perfect." He grabbed my jaw and gave me an intoxicating kiss that demanded every bit of my attention. He stole it with how he slid his tongue along mine, how he angled my head, how he moved his lips so fucking sensually, and how he controlled when I could come up for air.

When he lined up our bodies and tangled our legs, I had to bite back a moan. Feeling his cock against my own threatened to short-circuit my goddamn brain, and I couldn't stop from pressing myself harder against him.

He took a shuddering breath, then slid a hand between us, and I groaned under my breath as he palmed my cock.

He ghosted his lips over mine and spoke in a husky voice. "You don't know how liberating it is to touch you wherever I want."

I...uh. I was *pretty* sure I knew.

"I don't wanna laugh in your face, Boone." I smiled to keep it light, but he had to get one thing straight. "This is what I've wanted for most of my adult life." With that said, I took charge again. I shifted on top of him and pushed down his underwear, and mine followed. Other than an audible swallow of nervousness, he didn't express anything.

I ran my fingertips over his cock.

He cursed and shivered violently.

His cock was just like the rest of him, big and perfect, soft to the touch, rock hard underneath.

"God, that feels good," he exhaled.

"Let me swallow your cock, big brother," I whispered.

His breath stuttered. "Jesus. Okay." He nodded jerkily and scrubbed his hands over his face. "I-I might get rough."

Desire exploded within me. "Even better."

I didn't waste a second. I crawled down and got comfortable

so I could stroke myself off at the same time as I finally got my mouth on him, and he pushed himself up a little on his elbows.

His heated gaze was glued to me as I gripped the base of his cock and wrapped my lips around the head.

When I took him in, slowly, coating him with my tongue, he clenched his jaw.

"I didn't know this was what I wanted," he gritted out under his breath. "I feel like a caged animal—I don't wanna hurt you."

He couldn't. He seriously couldn't. But sensing his frustration, I made it clear I had no intention of teasing him or revving him up unnecessarily. I just wanted to take care of him properly —and give him everything. I sucked him long and hard, reveling in every goddamn second, and never before had giving someone else head offered *me* this kind of pleasure. The relief ran through me and didn't seem to stop.

"Fucking hell, Case." He struggled to keep his voice down, not to mention to keep his breathing even. "Oh fuck—oh fuck."

I closed my eyes and hollowed out my cheeks every time I sucked him in. Fisting my own cock, I went deeper until I had to fight against the urge to gag. Instead, I swallowed around his head and released the base of him. I wanted him to feel free to fuck my throat, so I pressed a hand underneath him instead, encouraging him to move.

He breathed harshly through his nose and shook his head. "I can't. Sit up. I gotta stand."

Fuck yes.

I eased back on my heels and wiped my mouth, then threw a quick glance toward the bed. Okay, good, we were safe. On the off chance that she woke up, she wouldn't be able to see us right away.

Boone's thoughts were similar to mine, and he moved closer to the corner of the couch where we'd be hidden further.

As I sat down on the edge, he reached down and wrapped

his fingers around my cock, and he captured my mouth in a brutal kiss.

I swallowed a groan at the pleasure coursing through me.

"Closer isn't close enough either," he rasped.

"I know." I kissed him swiftly, losing my patience. I had to get my mouth on him again. "Lemme go." I batted away his hand and gripped myself tightly, and he took the hint and shifted closer. He was a fucking vision in the pre-dawn light. Immense and powerful. Thick, muscular thighs, a big, hard cock, tight, heavy balls full of come that I wanted my mouth flooded with. "Don't hold back."

I didn't look away from him for a second as I sucked him in again, and I wanted him to watch the whole time. I wanted him to know who was getting him off, whose throat he was about to fuck.

There was less trepidation from him this time. It was so fucking hot how he controlled my movements, both hands on my head, and how he forced his cock deeper down my throat.

When I choked around him, his predatory gaze flooded with affection, and he touched my cheek almost reverently. And kept fucking me. It was gonna get me off faster than my own hand.

"You did this to me, little brother," he whispered roughly. "Now I won't be able to stop."

I moaned around him and felt myself spiral out of control. Sharp bolts of euphoria shot their way to every pleasure point in my body, and it was like coming to life. In that moment, I existed only for him, a thought that shoved me violently toward my orgasm.

"Don't come in your hand," he panted. "I wanna see it."

Oh God.

I couldn't hold it any longer. I screwed my eyes shut and jerked my cock quickly, and I tightened my lips around him. My eyes stung behind closed lids, my lungs burned, and my whole body ignited.

My heart pounded furiously.

Boone came without a warning. He rocked forward with a stuttered groan, pushing his cock along the roof of my mouth and down my throat, and then hot spurts of come started shooting out of him, causing his cock to throb in my mouth. It became my undoing. The climax hit me so hard that I had to lock my jaw into place so I didn't bite down. Release after release splashed onto the carpet between Boone's legs, and they took my energy with them.

He left me feeling raw and used in the best fucking way, and it seemed he wasn't done. He withdrew slowly from my mouth and then rubbed the wet, salty head of his cock across my lips.

I shuddered and hauled in a hoarse breath.

He towered over me, pushed me back against the cushions, and kissed me.

All I could do was pant and try to calm the fuck down, all while he manhandled me into whatever position he wanted me in. Back under the duvet, I discovered. It was messy. We were a pile of limbs, heaving chests, labored breaths, and wild kisses. His every move was an attempt to get closer, and instead of feeling suffocated, I took so much comfort in it. Whatever he wasn't ready to say verbally, his body took care of. Maybe this would end in broken hearts; I didn't care. Because he would never hurt me intentionally, and I couldn't ask for more.

"Wait," I croaked, breaking away from the kiss. I had to breathe. Christ, I was seeing black spots.

He didn't exactly *wait*. He just refocused his attention for a beat. He captured my bottom lip between his teeth and swiped his tongue over it, then kissed his way down to my neck, and he hugged me to him with a force only he possessed.

It melted me. It was a little funny too. "I'm not going anywhere."

He reemerged from the crook of my neck and furrowed his brow. "I gotta make sure. You're so tiny that a wind could—"

"Idiot." I punched his arm.

He grinned. It was one of his carefree, gorgeous, all-is-right-in-the-world grins that reached his eyes.

I smiled back and drew my fingers through his beard. "You need a trim soon."

"Mm." He dipped down and kissed me softly. "I guess we should get some more sleep before the hurricane wakes up."

Definitely.

I sighed. "I should do something about the mess I left on the floor first."

"Or we accidentally spill some Coke on the carpet, cover it in toilet paper, and leave it for housekeeping."

I rumbled a laugh and slipped my leg over his hip. "Your idea wins again."

TEN

Holy fuck.
  And I still wanted to get closer...
  I had to rethink some shit about my sexuality.

It took me four days to produce enough evidence against the wife who was cheating on Allegra's...whatever the man was. The woman was anything but subtle, and she seemed to have a sexual appetite that rivaled mine after I'd discovered masturbation.

When she wasn't getting banged by her tennis instructor, she was hooking up with her gardener and, as I discovered yesterday, one of her girlfriends. Although, I didn't have evidence she did anything with her friend that went beyond a make-out session. I'd caught them on camera when they'd left a restaurant to go their separate ways.

Thank fuck I hadn't been cheap when I'd bought my camera, because Ace was too curious for her own good. I'd brought her along after picking her up from school one day, and if I'd been forced to park close to wherever the woman flaunted her infidelity, my daughter would've had questions. Instead, I was able to say I was taking pictures of locations for Darius.

With the photographic evidence in hand, I met up with Allegra again, who was more than happy to hand over the information I wanted. Judging by the smug little smirk on her face, she was going to have fun breaking up a marriage.

I made my way home again, and Boone and I spent the next several days fleshing out all the details, reporting to Darius and Willow, and setting up a timeline for the Lange party.

On one Friday afternoon, after dropping off Ace at Ma's place, Boone and I brought Chinese food back to what'd somehow become *our* home, and we pinned the printouts of our remaining tasks to the wall in the living room.

We needed some child-free work time this weekend to decide where to go next.

I unwrapped my chopsticks and dumped rice into my serving of the best pork in Vegas. Deep-fried, sticky, sweet, spicy as fuck.

"How long can we postpone breaking in to AJ's house?" Boone asked.

"Not much longer," I replied, shoveling some food into my mouth. "I think we should go for Sunday." I stepped closer to the wall and pointed my chopsticks at AJ's well-established schedule. The man lived by a strict routine, which definitely worked in our favor. "We know he'll be gone for three hours from noon."

Breaking in during the day had some benefits. People weren't alarmed by activity when the sun was up, for one.

Boone had been able to find out a great deal about AJ's security. In this town, connections were everything, and we'd been around a minute. Thanks to a buddy, we had an educated guess on what to expect inside AJ's estate. Cameras outside but not indoors. Motion sensors out front but not in the back. And the aforementioned buddy was going to help us turn off the security alarm once we were inside.

"It's gonna be difficult not to take anything," Boone grumbled.

I grinned and snatched up a spring roll from another container. "We'll get our shot."

This time, we were only looking for information and clues, and we had to secure a safe entry in case Darius and his crew needed access. Boone and I would go in once the whole thing was over and rob AJ blind, at which point we'd been told by our cousin that AJ wouldn't even be around. I hadn't asked if AJ was going to end up in prison or in the desert—it didn't matter to me.

"All right, so Sunday's settled," Boone said. "We gotta do something about the anomaly in AJ's daily routine."

I nodded and shifted my gaze to the printout of a satellite image on the wall. In the weeks we'd run surveillance on AJ Lange, we learned he went to very few places. Work, golf course, gym, home, and the occasional restaurant. But last week, he'd driven out to a secluded address where a brothel once had been located. It was shut down now, though. Willow was currently trying to find an owner.

"We'll see if we find any information at his house," I decided. "Then we'll head out there—regardless of what we find

—next week." I narrowed my eyes on the list of AJ's various locations—and considering he didn't seem to have much of a social life, I was willing to bet he ran a lot of his interactions through safe channels online. "I wish we knew who he's met up with the few times he's gone out to dinner." We hadn't had the time to pursue any leads other than knowing the exact locations he'd parked and where he'd used valet service. We had to prioritize whatever was going on around his house. We knew when groceries were delivered and when his cleaning service showed up.

Boone picked up the tablet we'd been using to keep tabs. "Maybe we can find out. We still have one more week, don't we?"

I nodded.

"Well, we don't have too much on our plate after the weekend," he went on. "We can squeeze in a couple stakeouts."

True. And it would help. Because AJ was just a couple weeks away from having his family and his father's crime organization invade Las Vegas, and *someone* out there was running their errands—and it wasn't him.

It wasn't Allegra or the Langes' personal hospitality manager either. We'd combed through everything Allegra had given us, and while the info was great to have—it answered a shitload of questions—it provided us no clues that we could follow up on before guests arrived. Same with the hospitality guy, Oliver Hansen. Though, the last one could change. From what Laney and Allegra could tell us, we'd learned Hansen was a well-mannered but "kinda introspective and quiet" fella. He apparently did much of his work from home, meaning it was on our list. We knew where he lived and his work hours. Boone and I had to visit his place when he wasn't there.

I scratched my forehead, thinking on what Boone had said.

Maybe we didn't have too much on our plate next week, but we'd essentially saved the biggest operations for last.

"I think we need to split up," I said. "You can do the stake-outs—I'll pay Hansen a visit."

He frowned and glanced up from the iPad. "I don't want you to go without me. What if you need backup?"

"It's bad enough that we gotta work together to get into AJ's house," I replied. "This ain't our usual MO, Boone. You know that."

If we'd had more time, I would've preferred we split up a lot more. Like the president and the VP, we'd always tried to work separately for shit that could land our asses in prison. Breaking and entering was one of those gigs. Back in the day before we had Ace, we hadn't been as careful, and we'd also served some time for it.

Boone sighed, appearing irritated, and sat down on the couch. "Maybe I'd be on board if you weren't trying to push me away."

What the fuck?

"Excuse me?"

He threw me a bitchy look. "Don't pretend you don't know what I'm talking about. You've been different since the Venetian."

I *didn't* know what he was talking about, and I knew it showed on my face. In fact, he was fucking ridiculous, and that probably showed too. He'd basically moved in to my house the minute we'd left the hotel, and we'd spent every night together since. *Not* sleeping. My brother was all about hands and mouth, and I'd promised not to push him, no matter how badly I wanted to fuck him and get screwed in return.

"Have you lost your goddamn marbles?" I asked incredulously. "We're together day and night. The only time we're careful is when we're around Ace and Mom."

"But you barely take the initiative!" he argued. "If you're in the kitchen, I come in and act all sweet. If you're in the shower, I join you. When we go to bed, I'm the one who makes the move, and—why the fuck are you smiling?" he growled.

I couldn't help it! He was being cute.

After setting down my food on the coffee table, I went to him and straddled his whiny ass, ready to give him a piece of my mind. And he did the thing where he tried to be all indifferent, leaning back against the cushions, folding his arms over his chest, jaw set, stubbornness written across his features.

"Quit actin' like a child." I cupped his cheeks and made him look me in the eye. "It's been you and me for thirty-five years— as brothers and best friends. And whatever's going through your head might've been building up for who knows how long, but for *me*, your sudden interest in kissing and getting off together happened overnight." I couldn't stress that enough. "I don't know if you're going through a phase, if you're clinging to me because we just spent the last four years apart, or—"

"It's not a goddamn phase," he bit out.

I suppressed a sigh. "Okay. But you're missing my point. I don't know what the fuck is going on up here." I tapped the side of his head. "You don't wanna talk about it—you don't want me to ask questions. Well, then you're gonna have to calm your fucking tits and understand why I'm being careful. Because *I* know how I feel, Boone. I know that I will be a wreck once you figure out that all you really wanted was to secure a place in my life again."

We all did stupid things when we were desperate.

Boone glanced up at me with a scowl. "I thought you were supposed to be the smart one. In what universe would I believe I gotta suck you off in order to be part of your life?"

Oh, for chrissakes. I rolled my eyes and shifted off his lap. My back hit the armrest, and I leaned my elbows on it. "Try to think a bit further than that, *dick*. I confessed to you that I walked out because I had feelings for you, and how do you respond in your grief—to use your words—from missing me? You stick your tongue down my throat. What the fresh hell am I supposed to think?"

He averted his gaze and bit at a cuticle, but then his forehead creased and he glanced back at me. "First time I planted one on you was before any confession."

Was it? Oh. Maybe so. To be honest, I'd done my best to just shove that memory out of my mind, because none of it had made sense.

"Whatever—there's the nightclub too," I pointed out.

He shook his head. "Don't do that, Case. You're actively trying to minimize shit now. You *know* me. I'm a lot of things, but shifty ain't one of them. Not to you—not to family."

"Except for when you know I'm on my way home and you feel like getting head from the neighbor."

That remark earned me a glare, but I couldn't fucking help it. Sometimes I was still bitter.

He sat on all the answers, yet he demanded patience from me. He wanted to live with me, explore with me—or whatever it was—and now I was apparently not living up to the hype. I wasn't taking initiative. Fuck him.

"That was uncalled for," he told me.

"Was it?" I shrugged and got off the couch, wanting some distance. "Even though you didn't know back then why I didn't wanna see you with other women, you knew I was serious. I begged and fucking pleaded with you to just make that promise. And the last time, it wasn't some drunken mistake—you called that bitch over, fully aware that I was gonna walk in on you."

He flinched. "And I apologized— Hey, where are you going? We're in the middle of a conversation."

"I want a goddamn Pop-Tart," I snapped. "Is that okay with you?"

"No, we're gonna talk about this!"

Oh, so now he wanted to talk. How convenient for him.

"Blow me, Boone," I said on the way into the kitchen. "Or better yet, try the neighbor."

"Fuck you," he spat out.

"Not in your wildest dreams, sugar tits!" It was easy to mask my anger with laughter. I'd done it for years. Whenever he got smashed and sought out a pair of breasts to get lost in, I'd laughed and wished him a happy hunt.

I swallowed the ancient hurt that threatened to resurface and opened the cupboard. I didn't even want the damn Pop-Tart. I just needed space.

Since when did I get what I wanted, though? As soon as I heard Boone getting off the couch, I knew our fight was about to level up, and I steeled myself.

"Ask me why I did what I did back then," he demanded, appearing in the doorway.

I didn't spare him a single glance. "You can't even say it?" I snorted and popped two Pop-Tarts into the toaster.

"Ask me," he gritted out.

"No," I snapped irritably. "You're *done* always getting your way, and you can get the fuck outta my face or move back in with Ma. Those are your only options."

He completely ignored me. "You think that little of me, huh? Because the way I see it, you gotta think I'd be out to actually hurt you. Is that it? You honestly believe I'm that malicious?"

"I already know your excuse." I threw him a glare. "You were thinking with your dick—I've heard it before."

"That's not what I asked." He glared right back, and it made me wanna punch him in the face. He had no goddamn reason to be mad at me. "I wanna know what you believe, Casey. Do you think I would ever willingly hurt you?"

That set me off, and my blood went from simmer to boil in an instant. "How the fuck else am I supposed to interpret what you did, Boone?! You gave me your word and took a dump all over it!"

"Because I didn't know what you were going through!" he shouted. "I had no reason to think anything was wrong—other than you being a controlling piece of shit as usual!"

My eyes nearly bugged out, and I didn't know what to do with myself. His words slashed through me, hurting me as much as they infuriated me, and what killed me the most was that he was right. I'd been so fucking controlling back then, because I hadn't been able to keep my jealousy in check.

I felt the embarrassment rise under my skin, and it only made me angrier.

"So you thought revenge was best served with a woman's mouth on your cock," I said hoarsely.

"No." He swallowed hard, stewing, clenching his jaw, eyes brimming with anger and—something else. Defeat? "I thought it was the best course of action to make sure you didn't find out how fucking obsessed with you I was."

"You—" Wait, *what*? A breath gusted out of me, and I just stared at him.

Confusion numbed my brain, and the only thing I registered for several beats was the pop from the toaster when my Pop-Tarts were done.

I swallowed against the dryness in my throat.

Boone shifted from one foot to the other and dragged a hand over his face. "I didn't know what it meant back then." His voice came out like he'd been smoking and drinking all day. "I remember being so damn angry. You kept wanting me near you, and I lived for those days. At the same time, if I caught you in a bad mood, you were talking about—maybe it wasn't a good idea we lived together. So I was on pins and needles, just waiting for you to tell me it was time we went our separate ways."

He punched the fight out of me with those words, replacing it with a massive pile of guilt.

"I didn't want you to think I couldn't cope without you," he admitted. "Or that I had any other unhealthy attachment to you, so..."

Jesus Christ. What a perfect storm we'd created.

"I know I'm dumb sometimes." He cleared his throat, and I instantly wanted to put those words back into his mouth. "But I would never intentionally hurt you, Case."

I coughed into my fist, taken aback by a sudden onslaught of emotion. First things first, though. "That's the last time you say that shit. I can call you dumb, because I don't actually mean it. You can't."

He lifted a shoulder in a slight shrug. "Doesn't erase the fact that I've needed almost a decade to figure out what I feel for you," he said quietly. "It was easier with women. I know what it is about them I'm attracted to. With you, I...I could never pin it down."

I swallowed uneasily and folded my arms over my chest.

"When you said we were done, I stopped trying," he went on. "I convinced myself that I was just missing you—that it hurt because I wasn't part of your life anymore. And it worked for few years. Somewhat. I mean, I couldn't shake the grief, but at least I could function like a normal human being most of the time. I could be there for Ace. I met up with friends every now and then, and I worked. Which is pretty much how I spent these past four years." He took a break there, and I could tell he was struggling. He wouldn't look me in the eye. "I started feeling worse before I saw you with the guy you were dating, but something in me snapped that day. I fuckin' lost it. I became miserable."

So that was when his depression or whatever had started?

With my internal armor powered down again, I felt less defensive and could think clearly. It'd been wrong of me to place all the blame on him and, most of all, make him think I believed he wanted to hurt me. It was so far from the truth.

I reached out to him and grabbed his hand, and I pulled him toward me.

The moment I got my arms around him, he let out a shuddering breath and buried his face against my neck.

"I know you wouldn't hurt me intentionally," I murmured. "I'm a dick."

He sniffled and wrapped his arms around my neck.

"And I'm sorry I can be a controlling piece of shit," I added.

He let out a tearful chuckle and shook his head. "Didn't you hear what I said? I loved it when you got all bossy and demanded I should be by your side."

The fucker was gonna make me mushy too. That was usually his job, to be sweet and occasionally emotional. I was the hotheaded and sometimes catty asshole.

"The part where I was a piece of shit confused me." I smiled and dropped my forehead to his shoulder.

"Yeah, well. You can be both," he muttered. "You should crank up the possessiveness now, though. I miss it."

He was gonna be the end of me.

"You know that's not normally a healthy trait in any kind of relationship, right?"

"We ain't normal, Case." He eased back enough to meet my gaze.

Fucking hell, he was gorgeous. I reached up and wiped my thumbs under his eyes.

"There was one thing I was always sure of," he murmured. "And it kinda made me even more confused."

"What was that?"

He cleared his throat and flicked his gaze to my shoulder for a quick moment. "Even when I couldn't figure out if I was attracted to you or what the hell was going on with me, my obsession with you made it crystal clear that my life is nothing without you in it. It's fucking embarrassing."

What the— He had to ruin it. "I was getting ready to throw myself at you, until you said it was embarrassing."

He smiled ruefully and rested his forehead to mine. "Fine. You want the sappy, unfiltered truth? I've been pushed through a proverbial meat grinder these past four years, and I took the first easy breath a few weeks ago when we buried the hatchet." He palmed my cheeks. "Life without you is just survival."

I bit my lip in a weak-ass attempt to hide my grin. "That's much better. Now you just gotta figure out that you're attracted to me and prefer me over all the women on the planet."

He chuckled under his breath and ghosted his lips across mine. "Oh, I figured that out already—somewhere between fantasizing about raw-doggin' you and comin' on your face."

I spluttered a laugh and had to kiss him—hard. "That's the sweetest thing anyone's ever said to me."

He smiled against my lips, and it felt so fucking good when the tips of our tongues met and we eased into a deep, hungry kiss that closed an old chapter and opened a new one.

"I'm sorry I hurt you back then," I mumbled into the kiss. "Running hot and cold, I mean."

He hummed. "I'm sorry too." He brushed his thumbs over my cheeks and inched away slightly. "I want you to know I wasn't trying to drag this out. I was gonna talk to you about everything soon—but I got uncertain when it felt like you were pulling away. I need you to be as obsessed as I am."

"Baby, I'll fucking suffocate you if that's what you want. You've owned me since we were kids."

His eyes lit up with humor and affection. "Now we're talkin'."

We met in another kiss, and I got my arms around his neck instead so I could press myself closer to him. It was always where I wanted to be, impossibly close, and this time, I had no intention of stopping. No more holding back, trying to protect myself. He'd get all of me.

ELEVEN

Understanding the feelings I was harboring for the man who'd been my brother since I was a kid didn't just show me the future I wanted. It opened up the floodgates to every urge I'd suppressed throughout my adulthood.

I wanted the world to know he was mine.

I hissed as he sucked on my neck and rubbed my cock through my jeans, which were in the fucking way.

"You're not gonna make me wait any longer, are you?" I started pushing off his open shirt. I wanted him in just the beater with his jeans around his hips while he shoved his cock in and out of me.

He shook his head and captured my mouth in a bruising kiss, and he unzipped my jeans. "Couch?"

"Too far away." I needed him to take me right here.

"Fuck," he whispered, wrapping his fingers around my cock. "Then bend over for me, little brother."

I swallowed a moan and bucked into his hand, and I reached blindly for the olive oil I kept on the counter. Not optimal, not bad. Desperate times and all. I finally found the bottle and handed it over to him, and he raised a brow and took a step back.

"Just do it," I demanded. "I'm not exactly a virgin, and I want it to sting."

For some reason, that irritated him. "I don't wanna discuss your manwhoring days, Case."

I sucked my teeth and pulled my tee over my head. "Fuck you, I'm tight. I just mean this ain't my first time, and I know what I like." Besides, did he think a dick was the only action my ass saw? I was a pro with toys and fingers.

"I wasn't impl— You know what, we can bitch another time. Turn around."

Maybe this was better. Boone had his hotheaded moments too, and I bet annoying him would turn him into a rough motherfucker.

Once I had my back to him, he pushed down my jeans and my boxers with one hand, presumably using the other to slick up his cock. I braced myself against the counter and glanced back over my shoulder.

"I kinda like fighting with you."

"I fuckin' noticed." He kept his stare downward, at his cock, at my ass, while he rubbed in the oil. "God forbid we say something sweet to each other. Maybe you've got intimacy issues?"

I barked out a laugh. Less than ten minutes ago, we'd basically declared a mutual obsession with each other, *and* I'd used a term of endearment on my own brother.

"You need a job," I replied. "Sleeping on Ma's couch and watching *Dr. Phil* all day doesn't suit you."

"Oh, shut the *fuck up*, princess." Without another word, he pressed the head of his cock against my ass, gripped my hips, and tore me a new one.

Sweet-mother-of-God, it felt that way. I gnashed my teeth and banged my fist against the countertop at the pain that blazed through me. A whimper slipped from my lips. Kill me, he was all in. Holy shit. All the way in. In a single thrust, he'd buried his monster cock in my Kegel-certified asshole, and now I couldn't breathe.

"Are you okay?" Boone chuckled through a lust-filled groan. "Fucking hell, you weren't lying about being tight."

"I'm not sure it's true anymore," I wheezed out.

He rumbled a warm laugh and hugged me tightly from behind. Then he kissed my neck, each brush of his lips wiping away the traces of humor, and let his hands roam my chest.

I shuddered. A slow, white-hot wave of pleasure rolled over me, and I was left with a soaring sensation spurred on by a small voice at the back of my head that whispered, "He's inside me, he's fucking me, he's taking me," over and over.

I gasped raggedly once the initial burn started to fade, only to moan when he pulled out and pushed in again.

"That sound—when you moan..." He ground his pelvis against me to get deeper and grazed his teeth along my neck. A shiver ripped down my spine, and I couldn't help but push back. "I wanna hear it every day for the rest of my life."

Jesus.

I turned my head and met him in a messy kiss, and then I felt his fingers brush up the length of my cock. I groaned when he started stroking me, and I had a feeling it wouldn't take me long to get off. Fuck, he was intense. Overpowering. The way he manipulated my body was mildly terrifying, and I hoped I had the same effect on him. I fucking better.

I took over after a while so he could focus on screwing me into next week. The urgency in his pace, in his hold on me, and in his breath became my fuel. I met every thrust and drowned in the fiery pleasure. Pleasure with a sharp bite—nothing could top that.

He growled a curse as he slammed into me, shoving me up against the counter, and sank his teeth into my shoulder.

My God, I was a pain slut. The fire from tiny razors that'd been dipped in lava spread within, and I succumbed to it. In that moment, my body obeyed only his command. The sensations he fucked into me consumed me completely.

I groaned and stroked myself faster.

He soothed the sting from his teeth by dropping an open-mouthed kiss over the bite. "Tell me who owns this tight ass now, Case."

"You," I exhaled.

"That's right." One of his hands slid along my chest, past my sternum, and up to my throat.

My eyes closed of their own volition. I just took whatever he gave me. I drowned in it, craved more of it. Until the buildup became too much and I went off. Jesus Christ, I could barely support my own weight. I was sucked into the euphoria, and Boone held me up. He murmured something in my ear when I started coming, and it took me a beat to decipher the words.

"All fucking mine, Case. Come for me. That's it. Keep coming."

I fell forward as he pounded my ass through his own orgasm, and it wasn't until my lungs began burning that I realized I wasn't even breathing. Or that I'd let go of my cock. I blinked and saw both my elbows on the countertop, and the remnants of my orgasm trickled down the shaft.

Boone grew still, except for his heaving chest. And one hand that came up to my cock. He stroked it lazily and rubbed his fingers over the come.

I drew a shaky breath and wished we were in bed. My knees were about to give out.

"I need to be carried to bed," I croaked.

He let out a breathless chuckle, and then he pulled out of me carefully.

I winced anyway. Fucking hell, my ass was raw.

Taking a step back, I surveyed the mess and felt a little proud of my artwork. I'd come both on the lower cupboard and on the countertop. Oh, and on my T-shirt on the floor too. Nice.

"Can we pour Coke over it and call housekeeping?" I asked, out of breath.

Boone smiled into the kiss he dropped at the back of my neck. "I'll take care of it. Then I want us under the covers."

Me too.

Before I squeezed past him, I leaned in and kissed him hard.

It earned me one of his carefree, a little dopey, sweet grins.

Then I made my way to the bathroom and washed up, tucked myself back into my boxer briefs, and righted my jeans.

With a glance in the bathroom mirror, I caught myself smiling like a lovesick idiot, and I guessed that was pretty accurate. A strange calm had washed over me lately, little by little, and I no longer felt the heavy sorrow or jealousy that'd been my companions for so long. Phantom stings still flared up when I thought back on certain memories, but I knew with every fiber of my being that those days were behind me.

Boone was *mine*. He had to be. Somehow, we were gonna make this work our way.

I left the bathroom and wondered if he'd be opposed to

taking the rest of the day off. Maybe we could heat up our Chinese food and sit on the porch, shoot the shit, have a couple beers... But before I could ask, my iPad started blaring in the living room, which could only mean one thing.

AJ Lange was on the move and had diverted from his usual routes.

"What's that?" Boone asked from the kitchen.

"The tracking app," I replied, picking up the tablet from the table. "I added AJ's regular routes to a list, and if he drives somewhere outside of that zone, I get an alert."

"Clever."

I chewed on the inside of my cheek and pulled up the GPS map on the app. Could he be heading for that shut-down brothel outside town again?

Hmm. Well, he was still in Vegas.

"Where is he?" Boone joined me in the living room.

"Near the airport," I said. "If we're smart, we follow him." Because maybe he was meeting up with someone or picking someone up from the airport, though he was still sticking to the interstate. But it really fucking bugged me that we had absolutely no other people to keep track of. Alfred Lange's big birthday bash was approaching fast, and yet all we had was his son. A son who was also the only one listed as a contact person in Allegra's contract with the family.

It didn't add up.

"I'm game. We barely ate our dinner, though," Boone said.

"We'll get something when we're out," I decided. "Lemme just grab some gear, and then we'll go."

"I swear, if you spill—" Boone gave me a warning look. "Stop treating my truck like a fucking disco."

I scowled and stopped moving to the song. We should've taken my car instead. Convertible didn't mean I didn't have a roof at all. But nooo, he'd insisted we take his truck, in which you weren't allowed to have fun.

Boone wasn't done. He switched to muttering like an old man. "I clearly didn't fuck you hard enough if you can bounce around like a coked-up toddler."

Fucking *rude*. My ass hurt plenty. He should be happy for me that I'd found an angle that didn't trigger my sphincter's PTSD.

"You just love to suck the fun out of everything." I closed my lips around my straw and drank from my milk shake.

"Ptcha." He shrugged. "It worked with you."

Hey. That was funny, but he wasn't worth my laughter. Not when he'd put dance restrictions on Roxette's "Joyride."

"Be glad I let you bring a CD." He lifted his binoculars and peered through them.

"Okay, commie." I shoved some fries into my mouth, then followed suit. If he was gonna be boring, I might as well focus solely on work. "My binoculars are cooler than yours, by the way." I looked through the scope and toward the end of the parking lot. They were still talking. Christ.

"The fuck they are," Boone retorted.

I ignored his bullshit and focused on AJ.

I'd followed him on the iPad while Boone had taken us straight to a drive-thru for stakeout burgers and shakes, and then we'd stopped for a moment because AJ had driven around in a strange pattern, never stopping for more than a few seconds. Until here. When he'd pulled into one of the massive parking lots near Hard Rock, we'd been quick to come here too, though we were keeping our distance, parking in a spot right at the exit. With countless cars between us and under the cloak of darkness, no way were we on his radar.

But something was—or someone. Because the way he'd driven before coming here led me to believe he'd been trying to make sure no one was following him.

I chewed noisily on another handful of fries and watched AJ talk to his mystery friend. Whoever it was, we were gonna follow after they parted ways.

"Can you knock that off?" Boone growled and smacked my arm.

I grinned despite the life-threatening pain he'd inflicted. "I'm just expressing how much I love you."

To my surprise, he didn't answer.

Work sucked me in again, thankfully. I'd taken all the photos I needed, so I concentrated on coming up with theories. The man AJ was talking to wore a hoodie, indicating he wasn't some fat cat living in a nice estate or penthouse. He drove an old F-150, and Boone would know more about that one.

"What generation do you think that Ford is?" I asked.

"I don't think. I know it's a ninth gen, introduced in '92," he replied. "Could be a '95, but I'm not sure. Either way, it goes for around four grand."

Made sense. So whoever AJ was meeting up with, we knew it was a low-man. An errand boy.

They were replaceable and, in my experience, not worth much, yet AJ had been talking to him for over twenty-five minutes now. Perhaps there were new instructions and orders given.

AJ was all business. Judging by his posture and mannerisms, he was a little paranoid too, though he hid it well. He'd looked around himself a few times, and he had impatience rolling off him. Checking his watch, shifting his weight, then straightening and squaring his shoulders, as if reminding himself not to show signs of weakness.

On the other hand, he couldn't be too worried. He'd shown

up in a nice suit, not in disguise, and he drove his own car, not a rental.

Black hair combed back. Features drawn tight. He came off steely yet uncomfortable. He'd inherited more attributes from his American father than his Korean mother.

Boone cleared his throat. "You mean you, uh...that you love me like a brother, right?"

What? *Oh.* Oh, so that's where his mind had gone.

I kept my amusement to myself and noticed that AJ and his friend looked like they were wrapping things up. "That's for me to know and you to find out," I answered. "Get ready to follow the Ford. I think they're about to leave." Lowering my binoculars again, I side-eyed my brother and sensed he wasn't satisfied with my response. At this point, I wasn't afraid to admit the depth of my feelings, but I didn't think he was there yet.

As he stewed in silence and got ready to follow our target, I decided to give him a little something. After all, he'd been so forthcoming and genuine today, and I wanted to reassure him.

I skipped to track sixteen on the stereo and let the sweet notes of Savage Garden's "Truly Madly Deeply" pour out of the speakers.

Don't ever fucking tell me I wasn't romantic.

Boone didn't say anything, but it looked like he was warming up and trying to hide a little smile.

We followed the low-man to a cheap motel south of Winchester, coincidentally close to our third least favorite Denny's in town. Man, they'd fucked up my food bad that one time we went there.

The roadside motel catered mostly to long-term residents and had a partially broken-down sign that boasted of their continental buffet, and I didn't even know what that meant. Continental breakfast was toast and coffee, wasn't it? And a buffet was a buffet.

"You think he's in for the night?" Boone leaned forward and peered up toward the second and top floor of the motel.

"Probably." I eyed the cars around me again. One looked like it could be a rental. The rest were shitty rust buckets.

"So what do you wanna do now?" he asked.

"I'm gonna send the information to Willow." I pulled out my laptop from the bag at my feet and set it on my lap. "Maybe she can get access to the guests' files—fuck if I know. But I don't think we'll learn much by sticking around." And one more thing. "André should be able to give us some information from the license plate too." Always good to have a friend on the police force.

"In other words, I can take us home again," Boone finished.

I nodded absently as I typed out my message to Willow.

I was glad we weren't turning this into an all-nighter of work, 'cause we had to get up at the ass-crack of dawn tomorrow for Ace's soccer game.

Oh shit, good thing I thought of that now. "Remind me to unpack the new tees I ordered when we get home," I said. "I want us to wear them tomorrow for Ace's game."

"Yeah? What do they say?"

He knew me well. Ace had inherited her love for personalizing clothing items from me.

"Member of Ace O'Sullivan's Fan Club," I answered. "I got one for Mom too."

Boone chuckled. "Solid. I'm happy to finally be included."

I felt my forehead crease, and I side-eyed him in question. As far as I knew, he'd been a member of Ace's fan club as long as I had.

He shrugged. "I was dead to you when you started printing shit on clothes for you and Ace, and maybe I've been jealous."

"Just maybe?" I smirked, shaking my head. "Like you don't have your own traditions with her. I can't even take her to the movies without her making sure it's not a franchise she's following with you."

"We were talking about you, not me," he responded coolly. "This isn't some contest—or a joke. It's about you and me establishing the fact that I'm nice and innocent and you're a vicious man-eater."

I barked out a laugh, then snapped my teeth at him.

He'd see the real joke tomorrow morning when I gave him his new XXXXXL fan club tee. He'd glare at me, I'd laugh my ass off, and then I'd give him the real one in XXXL before we were off.

TWELVE

"Are you just not gonna talk to me?"

Not at the moment. I pulled into the drive-through and decided not to ask him what he wanted. "Yeah, hi, can I get two medium black coffees and a dozen original glazed? Actually, make four of them raspberry jelly."

"Anything else, sir?"

"No, I'm good. My brother already thinks I'm fat," I replied.

"Oh for fuck's sake," Case exclaimed. "It was a joke!"

Like I didn't know. I was just fucking with him. He wasn't the only one who could be a dick.

"**M**om's over there." I pointed toward the field.

Boone grunted and picked up our cooler to carry it on his shoulder, and I grabbed our chairs and a bag and led the way. It was gonna be a hot-as-balls day, and part of me hoped Ace's team got eliminated fast. Not that I'd ever admit that shit.

There was no denying I preferred single games at her school over these hooplas, though. Ten teams were facing off today, and if Ace's team played like she did, we'd be here all day. Ten teams, four soccer fields, countless family members, music, and 109 degrees.

I didn't know where the music was coming from, but I appreciated it.

As we got closer to the field where Ace would play her first game, I spotted her warming up with her friends.

My heart clenched at the sight of her. Mom must've braided her hair already.

"Ma!" Boone hollered.

Mom glanced over at us and rose from her chair. She'd dyed her hair again. Brown was better than ketchup red.

She grinned at our fantastic T-shirts. Plain white tees with black text, because I didn't wanna steal focus from the message.

"Look at you boys," she gushed. "I'm so glad you made up."

Boone and I exchanged a smirk.

Then I dipped down and kissed her cheek and told her I had a tee for her too. "And snacks. We got you wine and cheese."

"Oooh, fancy. Thank you, sugar. I brought sandwiches and cookies for us." She directed where I could place the chairs, and I did an internal fist-pump. Her sandwiches were the best. Boone and I had only brought beer, a couple bags of chips, the wine and cheese for Ma, leftover Chinese food, a bag of gummy worms, some Slim Jims, jerky, three slices of questionable pizza I'd found in the fridge, water, a box of Twinkies, and the coffee and dozen donuts we'd bought on the way.

"Ma, did you make mine with meatballs?" Boone questioned. "The ones you make yourself?"

"Of course, baby." Mom took her seat again.

My brother whispered a "Fuck yes" and plopped down next to her, the chair creaking at the impact.

I kept my amusement to myself as I fanned out the XXXXXL T-shirt between our chairs. It could be Ace's blanket when she was allowed to come over for a break.

Boone shot me a scowl before seeking support from Mom. "Look what he did. He thought it'd be fun to make us these shirts, but not before bullying me viciously."

Mom leaned forward and eyed the tee on the grass. She sniggered. "And I'm sure you didn't punch your brother in return."

"He totally did!" I exclaimed. "My shoulder still hurts."

"Oh, cry me a fucking river," Boone huffed. "No one cares about me."

Who was crying a river, really?

"That's enough," Mom told him. "You're equally cruel toward each other sometimes. The only difference is, Casey says it to your face, and you say shit behind his back."

"Whoa!" I stared at him, incredulous, while he got defensive.

"That was before!" he argued. "Way before, even—when I was pissed." He turned his glare on Mom. "How about you don't rehash old crap? He's still a flight risk, and I don't wanna get kicked out."

Hmpf. The fight left me, though I decided to put him on

probation. But no, I wasn't a fucking flight risk. He was being ridiculous. Maybe I wasn't the drama queen between the two of us after all. He seemed plenty dramatic to me.

"How about the two of you become nicer?" Mom retorted. "You still treat each other like you did when you were children. Casey throws insults, you throw punches. Just stop it. If you weren't brothers, I'd say you were both running around in a sandbox yanking each other's pigtails because you have a crush."

Welp.

Funny how quickly that shut us up.

It was something we had to discuss sooner rather than later. I couldn't foresee any major issues from our mother; not only was she open-minded, but she was used to us giving her gray hairs for one reason or another. And I didn't think us being a couple would top the two separate occasions we'd been to jail. Once for theft, where we'd served nine months together. Then I'd been arrested for assault one time, where the case had been dropped, and Boone had served three months for possession.

He'd brag about being released on good behavior, but we knew the reality was more an issue of overcrowded jails.

Either way, if Mom could handle all that, she could handle us being together.

The issue was Ace. Mom had legally adopted me, meaning we had to look into the state laws on incest and shit like that, because we wouldn't risk losing custody of our daughter. Even if there was a no-relation clause that made us exempt, which was likely the case, all it took was a badass prosecutor against a shitty defense, and we'd lose everything. I had zero faith in the legal system, and cops didn't like me for some weird reason.

I didn't know what brightened my day the most, watching my girl score twice before halftime of the first game or Mom's pastrami sandwich.

It was a toss-up.

"This was so fucking good, Ma." I crammed the last of it into my mouth and picked up my beer. Obviously, I had my pink koozie that solemnly swore it was just soda.

"I'm glad you liked it," she replied with a smile. "What about you, Boone?"

"Not enough mayo," he said with his mouth full. "But it was all right."

I frowned and reached over our cooler to smack his arm. "The fuck is wrong wit'chu? She worked hard on that. The last thing she needs is ungratefulness from your misogynistic ass." I knew the times we lived in. It was important to support our women. "Apologize and tell her to make you two sandwiches next time."

Boone winced and offered Ma an apologetic look. "I'm sorry —I did like it. Especially the roasted onion."

Ma took a deep breath, closed her eyes for a beat, and rubbed her temples.

It gave me an idea. I knew how to make it better. I opened the cooler and brought out the wine and cheese. "Here, Ma. This is for you." I got out of my chair to bring it to her. We'd emptied half a bottle of red into a Coke bottle, and the pack of string cheese was a nice brand and everything.

"It's from me too," Boone was quick to say.

I withheld my eye roll.

Mom accepted the gift and stared at it. "This is...so nice of you. Thank you, boys."

I smiled, satisfied, and returned to my chair and flipped open the box of donuts.

That evening, we invited Mom over for a barbecue. Since Ace was gonna spend the night with her again, I wanted our little soccer champion to spend some time with us at home before they were off again.

It'd been a great day. Ace was wearing a silver medal around her neck, and Boone and I were sporting impressive sunburns.

"This really turned out great, Casey." Mom was checking out my new porch from where she was sitting at the table.

"It did, didn't it?" I agreed with her. It wasn't very big, but I had enough room for a grill in the corner, a table for four, and a plastic chest at the other end for Ace's pool toys and the seat cushions. We didn't need more than that. But it was nice to get off the ground. We did get some snakes around here, and Ace was terrified of them.

Boone came out with an armful of condiments and more beers, Ace close behind with soda and paper plates.

I flipped the burgers on the grill and took a swig of my beer.

Boone sat down next to Ma, and he was watching Ace with a proud grin. "Lemme see that thing again, baby G." She was all too happy to join him. He turned the medal in his hand and shook his head. "You don't know how proud Daddy and I are. We should put up a shelf in your room for all your trophies."

That was a good idea. She'd earned a few by now.

Ace beamed. "I hope I get one more in November."

"For the spelling bee?" I asked.

She nodded and climbed up on Boone's lap. "The competition ain't lookin' too hot, son. S'all I'm sayin'."

I laughed.

Mom leaned back with a wry little smile. "Maybe this time, Boone can attend."

That made me snort. I wasn't banking on it. Last year, he'd

stood up in the auditorium and yelled "Boo, you S-U-C-K!" to the boy who lost to Ace. Even I had supported my brother's ban on that one.

"I didn't know spelling bees had so much suspense," Boone replied defensively. "Excuse me for getting excited. No one woulda batted an eyelash if it'd been football."

I mean...

"They're young children, Boone," Mom grated.

I shook my head in amusement, then plated the burgers and joined them at the table.

"Daddy, can I put on some music?" Ace asked me.

"Sure thing." I dug out my car keys and tossed them to her. "Remember not to turn the ignition this time."

She giggled and ran down the steps.

"Don't you have a ridiculously expensive stereo inside?" Mom asked.

"I ain't keeping the door open when the AC's runnin'," I replied. That was nuts.

She accepted that.

Conversation lulled while we prepared our burgers, and I got Ace's ready while listening for her in the carport. Knowing her, she was flipping through my CD case to find the perfect mix.

"I love the girl, but she wouldn't know a good burger if it smacked her in the face," Boone said.

I grinned and added another slice of cheddar. He had a point. I was on board with the plain buns without sesame seeds —I preferred those too—but the rest was just gross. Four slices of cheese, relish, and barbecue sauce. Or a Paisley Special, as we called it.

"We're alone, by the way," Ma filled in with. "You said you wanted to talk to me about something when she wasn't here."

Oh right. Now was as good a time as any, and it wouldn't take long.

"What's your schedule like these days?" I asked. "Your hours still flexible?"

She furrowed her brow. "Well, sure. Do you need me to watch Ace more?"

"Not just Ace," Boone replied. "Darius is coming to town soon, and he's bringing his sons."

I let him do the talking, partly because I was still mind-blown. Our recluse of a cousin, this badass former PMC who hated humanity and had always rejected the notion of kids, had switched teams and shacked up with a dude, and they had adopted two boys together.

I listened on one ear as Boone gave Mom the need-to-know level of details about Darius coming to town, and by the time I had made two burgers for myself, I wondered what was taking Ace so long.

"Get a move on, Paisley!" I hollered. "Your food's gonna get cold."

"I'm trying to decide!" she yelled back. "Would you say we have a 'Semi-Charmed Life'?"

I chuckled, biting into my burger.

Seconds later, music poured out from my car, followed by the door slamming shut and the alarm being activated. Around the same time, Ma was telling us that, of course, she'd be happy to watch Darius's kids, and the crease between her eyebrows told me she had questions. Many of them.

She was generally good at butting out—mainly 'cause she didn't wanna know—but she had limits, and this involved family. So I had to nip something in the bud.

"You can't call Aunt Mary about this," I said.

Her stare grew tight. "Why not? You're up to something big, aren't you?"

What a travesty that we couldn't respond, because Ace hopped up the porch steps and rejoined us.

This was a bad night to catch a sudden bout of insomnia.

I rolled onto my back and slipped my hands underneath my head, and I tried to match my breathing with Boone's. It usually soothed me. Never had I heard the fucker snore. He slept peacefully on his stomach, his back rising and falling with long, deep breaths.

I blinked drowsily and aimed my stare at the ceiling instead. Maybe I should buy curtains. Whenever someone moved outside, a carport or porch lit up.

The AC hummed steadily. In the bathroom, the faucet dripped every ten or eleven seconds. The fridge and freezer buzzed. Crickets competed to see who could piss me off first. Every now and then, a car drove past outside.

For as rambunctious as Boone and I had always been, we'd grown up chasing moments of silence, too. It'd started as soon as we got our driver's licenses. We'd drive straight out into the desert sometimes and just listen to nothing.

Some of my favorite memories were from when Boone had bought and repaired his first truck. Mom would pack us sandwiches and sodas, and we'd head out to sleep under the stars. Just the two of us in the bed of the truck. We'd lie there in our sleeping bags, passing a joint between us, and, for the most part, be absolutely quiet.

I missed that.

Sharing silence with someone could be incredibly intimate. At least for me.

I released a breath and scrubbed my hands over my face.

Sleep, goddammit. Sleep.

Big day tomorrow. Important day. Nothing was allowed to go wrong. I wasn't the slightest bit worried about breaking in to the hospitality guy's apartment next week, but this...? Fuck. AJ Lange liked his security.

Boone shifted next to me, causing the sheet to ride down when he twisted it around his leg. "Go to sleep, little brother."

Oh.

"I'm trying," I murmured. "Did I wake you?" I couldn't have.

"I don't know." He yawned and stretched out, then pushed himself up a bit on his elbow. "Maybe. I can sense when you're restless."

I scratched my jaw. My turn to need a trim soon. Boone had trimmed his this week. A little, anyway.

"I miss silence," I admitted.

He hummed quietly and moved closer. "We could go camping when all this is over."

I nodded and tilted my head to him. "Yeah. Sounds good." With him so close, I had to pull him in for a kiss.

He smiled faintly, his lips moving against mine with sleepy seductiveness. "Something else botherin' you? Something about tomorrow?"

"Nothing beyond regular jitters." I squirmed my way into his embrace and turned his arm into my pillow.

It was probably ridiculous, but it really felt like a dream come true every time he squeezed the shit out of me in one of his strong hugs. Having his big arms around me, being the center of his attention, eased the unrest within me.

There was no word that could do justice to how much I loved him.

"I wanna tell Mom about us soon," Boone murmured hesitantly.

I peered up at him and found him looking at me in a way

he'd done before. He was waiting for direction and approval. He wanted to know what I thought.

"We will." I brushed the pad of my thumb over his bottom lip. "Soon as this job's done—and once you've decided what you want us to tell her." I elaborated when I saw his brow furrowing. "We haven't established a relationship. I don't know exactly what it is you want. A regular relationship? You want us to show up at a game or recital hand in hand? Or do you want something more discreet?"

That made him frown. "I sure as fuck don't wanna hide. I thought we were on the same page and wanted the couple shit."

I chuckled and kissed him quickly. "I'm on that page. Just had to make sure you were on it too."

He hummed into the kiss, not entirely satisfied yet. "Fuck discreet," he muttered. "First time in my life, I wanna make an effort. Maybe I'm not good at romantic dinners, but I want an anniversary to celebrate and quick getaways for just you and me."

That sounded perfect to me. "You know what's a romantic meal to me? Sandwiches in the desert. Packed lunch on the beach. All-you-can-eat ribs in front of the TV. Chinese food in bed. Those are the only dates I'm interested in."

He smiled more genuinely and kissed me harder. "We're kinda perfect for each other."

"We kinda are." I grinned and leaned back against his bicep again, and I just looked up at him.

He combed back my hair with his fingers. "If I say something sweet, will you call me cheesy?"

"Absolutely," I promised.

He chuckled silently and dipped down, resting his forehead to mine. "You're beautiful, Case. Hot, fucking adorable, and so sexy that it drives me crazy."

Good luck wiping the grin off my face now. "Kiss me, you cheesy bastard."

Now I knew how I could fall asleep. He could fuck me into oblivion and exhaust my body.

THIRTEEN

Ma talking my ear off at seven in the morning wasn't exactly what I'd had in mind today. I adjusted the earbud and listened to her go on and on about the novel she was writing, but most of my focus remained on counting my sets.

I grunted and set down the kettlebell on the porch. The burn that coursed through my arms made me feel alive. It had the added bonus of Case getting turned on when he watched me lift, too. I'd heard him inside the trailer, so I knew he was awake.

"So what do you think?" Mom asked.

"I think it sounds great," I answered distractedly. I picked up the kettlebell with my other hand this time and began a new set of twenty. "Next bestseller."

Three, four, five...

I gnashed my teeth.

Case stepped out on the porch a few seconds later, a Pop-Tart trapped between his teeth, and one hand down his sweats, scratching his balls. I wanted them in my mouth. Or, lately, slapping against my ass.

"Mornin'." He pulled out a chair and sat down. "That's one sweaty bicep—that I kinda wanna lick."

I winked at him.

Mom kept rambling.

He nodded at my phone on the table, maybe since I hadn't given him a verbal response. "You talkin' to someone?"

"Mom," I mouthed.

"Ah." He sat back and took a bite of his Pop-Tart. "I guess it was okay when she cockblocked us in high school, but, uh, I'm about to hit the shower if you wanna join."

If I did?

"Ma, I love you, but I gotta go," I said and disconnected the call.

Now was not the time to get hungry. Not when we were parked on AJ's street, waiting for him to fuck off so we could break in to his house.

"Do you remember Mom's tomato soup?" I asked, attaching the mag to my gun. For emergencies only, of course. I'd just used it to shoot soda cans in the desert. Boone had used his to shoot himself in the leg once.

"With the rice?" he asked.

I nodded. Growing up, it'd been my favorite meal. Whenever we were sick or we'd just had a bad day, Ma would bake cheese-filled rolls and make her tomato soup with rice and cut-up hot dogs and bacon. To this day, it was the definition of comfort food.

"I remember our friends calling it weird," Boone said.

"I remember us kicking their asses for it," I replied with a smile.

He smirked.

"What about it?"

"It occurred to me that Ace has never tried it," I said. "When we pick her up tonight, we gotta get groceries anyway. We could find out the ingredients and make it for her." Perhaps we could do a movie night. I was itching for some family time.

"I'm game. But we're buying the bread. Unless—" The idea struck him probably at the same time as it struck me. He quickly retrieved his phone. "I'm texting Ma. Maybe she'll wanna bake for us."

Exactly.

I scratched my nose and checked the sideview mirror. Any moment now, we'd see AJ dumping his golf bag into his car.

Boone had borrowed us an inconspicuous car to blend in on the street, a nice white Acura sedan. Nobody gave a fuck about those. They weren't expensive enough to be noticed—or cheap enough to stick out like a sore thumb. It was just a car. A forgettable car.

"Ask if she wants to make cookies too," I said.

Boone nodded slowly, concentrating on typing.

I shifted in my seat and checked the time. Almost noon. Fuck, I just wanted to get this over with. Not only because I didn't like the risks that came with breaking in to rich folks' houses, but because my clothes were fucking uncomfortable.

The cargo pants in desert camo with side pockets worked—the ugly, skintight turtleneck, not so much. But it was the only item of clothing we could wear if we wanted to cover all our ink. On the off chance that someone saw us, there was no need to give them any recognizable marks to tell the cops about.

Lastly, our shoes. They were the worst touch. They were two sizes too large and added a couple inches to my height. Anything to confuse potential witnesses and investigators.

Movement caught my eye, and I glanced in the sideview mirror again. "He's on the move." My pulse thrummed a little faster as I watched AJ in his driveway.

I couldn't quite figure him out. He didn't strike me as an OCD type. Not a hair out of place, living on a strict schedule, his posture, the way he moved—always with a sense of purpose —no... If anything, he reminded me of our cousins. Someone with an extensive past in the military carried themselves a certain way.

I made a mental note to bring it up with Willow.

"We're gonna have to be really fucking careful here," I murmured, eyes still on AJ. "If he's anything like Darius, we're essentially walking into the lion's den."

"What makes you think he's like Darius?" Boone asked.

"I don't know." I frowned. "Just something about him."

AJ backed out of the driveway and drove off, and if all went according to plan, he wasn't coming back until later this afternoon.

"All right, let's get ready." I reached for my backpack in the back seat and scooted forward to put it on. Gloves followed. I had a whole box, courtesy of my tattoo artist. Black latex gloves.

"Jay's ready to cut the security alarm." Boone pocketed his phone, and I nodded in acknowledgment. Then he started the car and pulled out of the spot to find parking near the end of the street instead. There were four more houses after AJ's. "I've been thinking about ribs since you mentioned it last night."

"Fuck, bro, me too. We'll buy ribs on the way home."

"Deal."

Boone snagged the last parking spot before the cul-de-sac, and I glanced around us to make sure there weren't any nosy neighbors around. Noon on a Sunday, anything could happen. We were lucky that AJ lived on the edge of his neighborhood and that there was plenty of nothingness around us. In fact, on the map, his street poked out of Summerlin like a peninsula, with desert on two sides and a golf course to the south. Not the one where AJ was a member.

"All clear. Let's roll. Don't forget the iPad." I stepped out of the car and into the blistering heat. For chrissakes, the triple-digit temperatures should be over for the year by now.

Boone and I left the curb and headed down along the side of the last estate on the street. They'd opted for a six-foot-high stone wall, making us invisible on the outside. A stretch of desert extended between the property line and the golf course too, so at least we had nothing to worry about right here. The nearest golf cart I spotted looked more like a toy car.

Stone wall's neighbor had thick hedges, and the two houses after that, high picket fences.

We stopped right before AJ's house, and I pulled out my binoculars. He didn't have a high wall or fence, because he had an infinity pool. It was elevated to the height of my shoulders, though it wouldn't be difficult to ascend it. As long as we didn't tumble into the water.

I peered through the binoculars, starting with every corner on the exterior I could find. Under the balcony, along the terrace, near the roof of the estate. Just double-checking to make sure there weren't any hidden cameras.

"His car has been still for a few minutes now," Boone said. "Same spot as the other Sundays."

Good.

We *should* have at least four or five hours, because according to our digging around at the exclusive club he was a member of and tracking him for the past few weeks, he finished off his round with a drink or a meal at the club's restaurant, but it was better to play it safe. We'd only been able to follow AJ to the golf course one time, and we'd had to stay in the parking lot. We'd seen him enter the restaurant with two other men, typical white dudes with fat wallets and bellies, owners of a couple of the expensive cars in the lot. But AJ had reemerged to go home before the other two, and our time had run out. We'd never found out who he golfed with, if they were work friends or other associates. And with more than one loose variable, I wasn't taking chances. All it took was an angry wife or a work-related emergency for their Sunday fun to get cut short.

"See anything?" Boone asked.

I shook my head and refolded my binoculars, then tucked them back into one of the pockets. "We're good. Try not to fall into the water." No time to waste. I flattened my hands against the edge of the elevated pool and hoisted myself up with a grunt. *Whoa.* Water—right there. My nostrils filled with the smell of chlorine. "Edge's narrower than you think. Be careful."

A three-foot jump separated me from the outer edge of the pool to the nearest side where solid ground was. The entire pool area was lined with flagstone, including the "fence," which consisted of sheets of rock. But closer to the patio, a regular fence took over.

Boone heaved himself onto the edge once I'd cleared the spot, and my breath got stuck in my throat when it looked like he was about to roll into the pool. Man, it woulda been hysterical.

"Nailed it," he grunted.

I grinned and took a couple steps back so he could jump too.

He made a face and threw me his bag. "If I fall in, I'll never hear the end of it."

"I'm glad we're on the same page."

He blew out a breath, then took a big leap and, unfortunately, remained dry.

"Jesus. That's enough cardio for one day," he claimed, out of breath.

I snorted and started walking toward the house. My brother liked to say that cardio was for losers who couldn't lift a twenty-pound dumbbell. He hadn't complained last night, though, when he'd licked my abs, and I sure as fuck hadn't lifted much in my day. I liked to run, swim, row, and do sit-ups and chin-ups.

I also liked to pick locks, and this was the fun part. I was ready for whatever AJ would throw at me, dead bolts—single-cylinder or double—latches, digital locks, spring locks, whatever. I had the gear I needed in my backpack, including several bump keys, pins, a code scrambling device, and a high-voltage shocker that could short-circuit and reboot most smart locks.

As I climbed up the patio deck and passed the seating area, I dropped Boone's bag on the ground and removed my own. The floor-to-ceiling sliding doors revealed a sparsely decorated living room on the other side of the glass. I could see into the kitchen too. No surveillance indoors, thank fuck. And that was where the similarities between AJ Lange and my cousins ended. Darius and Ryan wouldn't be caught alive in a sterile environment like this. Why even have bookshelves if you didn't own books? Excuse me, there was a single stack of what appeared to be coffee table books on one shelf. The rest was overpriced knickknacks called art.

There had to be a rule somewhere about African art. It seemed so stereotypical. Nevertheless, for some unknown reason, AJ had a thin bronze statue of a giraffe between two chairs.

It was safe to say that AJ didn't have any kids in his social circle. 'Cause all I saw were hazards where Ace would've hurt herself as a toddler. From the sharp edges of the glass table to the staircase without a railing. The black steps shot out from the wall with nothing in between.

I shook my head and refocused. Down on one knee in front of the door, I inspected the lock and nodded to myself. I was gonna need about half an hour.

"What kind of lock is it?" Boone asked.

"Double-cylinder deadbolt," I replied, opening my backpack.

Boone hummed and disappeared from my periphery.

Okay, time to get down to business. I wanted Ace to be proud of me. We'd practiced this together a lot. I'd have a set of locks lined up on the coffee table at home, and she'd time me to see how quickly I could pick them.

I brought out my kit for deadbolts and—

"Or we can use this window over here," Boone said.

I felt my brows knit together and annoyance flare up. Windows were no fun at all. "What kind of lock is it?" There was a pillar in the way, preventing me from seeing the window in the first place.

Boone smirked. "I'm not sure it matters. It's open."

To hell with that!

"Are you fucking kidding me?" I snapped irritably. What kind of moron spent tens of thousands of dollars on security and left the goddamn window open? On the first floor! I rose from the ground and stalked over there, legitimately pissed. Not only because AJ was robbing me of the fun of putting my skills to use, but because this shit made me wary. It made no sense to leave a window open in this heat.

Fine if you were smoking a joint with your brother—you popped the window for a bit and then closed it again. You didn't fucking leave the house.

Sure enough, the window was ajar.

"I don't like this." I dug through my bag to fetch my modified pliers with extra-long grips. "What if it's a setup?"

"What're the odds of that?"

Fuck if I knew.

I found the pliers and handed the bag over to my brother. Then I snuck the pliers and my arm as far as they went, and I squirmed around a bit to reach the latch on the inside.

"I'll check the tablet and tell Jay to kill the alarm," Boone said.

I grunted in response, my arm twisting uncomfortably, and managed to turn the latch.

"He's still parked at the golf course," he told me.

Yeah, well. This was the type of crap that made me paranoid. What if he'd found the tracker? What if he'd left it at the golf course to catch us? He could be pulling into the driveway right now.

We'd just have to be more careful. If we left a room, we brought our shit with us, in case we had to make a quick exit.

A couple minutes later, I got the go-ahead from Boone's buddy. The security alarm would be off for the next two hours, and I didn't waste a second. I pushed myself up and climbed through the window, and I landed on a polished hardwood floor in front of the staircase.

I held my breath for a few seconds, all my focus on my surroundings. Not that I didn't trust this Jay guy, but...I didn't trust this Jay guy. I could hardly trust my brother when I was busy running paranoid fears through my brain.

So far, so good.

I removed my shoes, shut the window enough to turn the

latch again, then headed over to the patio doors where Boone waited with our gear.

As I let him in, I drew a deep breath and registered the faint smells of wood, soap, paint, and cigar.

"I'll start upstairs," I said quietly, shoving my shoes into my backpack. "You be on the lookout for anything strange down here. Holler if you see movement on the iPad."

"Of course. This isn't our first time, Case. We got this."

I nodded once. He was right.

After grabbing my bag, I went up the stairs and got my ducks in a row. AJ would have a home office somewhere; I was sure of it. And at the top of my list of shit to do was planting a transmitter in there so we could get an audio feed. My feet hit soft carpet on the second floor, and I looked around me.

Interesting—there was a cross breeze up here. More windows had to be open. Two doors to the left, three to the right. The latter three were fully open and revealed bedrooms, so I veered left and hit the jackpot on the first try. The door was already ajar, and I poked my head into the room.

This was an impressive office. *Damn.* The design was similar to the rest of the joint, sterile and trendy, but this was where AJ showed some personality. The wall behind his desk was filled to the very last slot with books. The wall across the room had a minor collection of photos.

Speaking of, I had to take pictures of everything. Details could be studied later when we were home again. But first things first. I retrieved my AirPods—or one of them—and inserted it so I could get some music. I worked better when I had good tunes accompanying me.

I pushed play on some sweet Redbone, then spent the next few minutes with my camera. I photographed the bookshelves, the family pictures, the furniture... Hmm. I paused at the coffee table between the two chairs and cocked my head. The image of

AJ Lange was becoming clearer. Tiny metal figurines in various martial arts poses stood on the table, and it wouldn't surprise me if AJ had training in that. In fact, it would make more sense than a past in the military.

Deciding that one of the chairs was a good place to get audio, I fished out the little transmitter and peeled off the adhesive film. Then I attached it to the underside of the leather chair, on the inside at the base of one of the legs.

I heard Boone coming up the stairs as I moved on to take more photos of the grand desk. It was the one piece of furniture that didn't fit in. There was nothing new and trendy about it. The opposite. It looked like it belonged in a dusty old English castle. Big and sturdy, dark wood, intricate details.

It'd be fun if there were any hidden drawers.

"You didn't run up the stairs, so I assume there's no immediate danger," I said, squatting down to peer under the desk.

"No, I think we're good," Boone replied. "There's an explanation for the open window."

"Oh yeah?"

"Yeah." He came over to me and handed me a note. "Found this on the kitchen counter."

I accepted the note and appreciated my brother's forethought—and thoroughness. There wasn't actually anything written on the note, but there'd been a message on the sheet above this one on the notepad, and Boone had used a pencil to give the paper a darker shade. It made it easier to see what AJ had written on another note.

I squinted.

It was addressed to an Irene, and it seemed... "Wait. Irene is from the maid service?"

"That's what it looks like to me too."

Huh. So AJ was on a first-name basis with the woman who cleaned here, and it looked like it was more than that. He sounded almost apologetic when mentioning he'd smoked a cigar in his study—but he'd left the windows open. That was hella interesting. We knew the cleaning service had been here yesterday—every Saturday at ten in the morning while AJ was at work. Because the guy didn't have a life.

There were instructions too, and it confirmed my suspicion about where AJ's parents were gonna stay. Irene was told to prepare the main guest room. Who else could it be for if not his folks?

"AJ's still at the golf course, so I thought I'd check out the guest rooms," Boone said. "There's nothing else to see downstairs. I took some photos."

"Okay, cool. Thanks." I handed the note back to him. "Save that."

He nodded and walked out.

Well, that was a relief. Even though it made me all the more curious. It appeared AJ *did* have a life; he just hid it very well.

I got behind the desk and sat down in the chair, and I started opening the drawers. There was surprisingly little inside them, so it wasn't difficult to put stuff back the way it was. Except... I sucked my teeth and stared at the second bundle of cash I'd seen in as many minutes. A handful of crumpled fifty-dollar bills. I knew I'd said we weren't taking anything this time around. We'd get our shot after Darius had taken over. But god*damn*.

My fingers got a little sticky.

I only took two bills. A hundred bucks was nothing. "Okay, back to work," I mumbled to myself.

More pictures. Now wasn't the time to read the folders that I flipped through—I only took pictures. All the pictures. And fuck, more money. Was he just throwing it in here? There were several hundred dollars in each drawer. *Focus on pictures!* And checking to see if there were any—fucking bingo! The bottom of the last drawer definitely had a secret compartment.

Getting down on one knee in front of the drawer, I carefully lifted the bottom and grinned. Score.

It wasn't money—or diamonds, for that matter—but if someone put something in a hidden compartment, it meant they didn't want anyone to see it. I retrieved the envelopes and opened them.

I furrowed my brow and tilted my head. Tiny photos, upside down. I took one out and—immediately felt nauseated. Holy fuck. Oh holy fucking shit.

You sick motherfucker.

I killed the music, then began emptying the envelopes on the desk, creating a picture grid from hell.

"Oi!" Boone hollered down the hall. "I found his safe in the walk-in in his bedroom."

"Be there in a minute," I answered absentmindedly. Not all the photos fit on the work surface. Far from it. There had to be over fifty in total. I had to call Darius. Right now. Swallowing the queasiness, I scrolled down to his number and called.

Jesus Christ, this was something else. Boone and I were no angels and rarely held the moral high ground, but this... Fuck me, it made me sick to my stomach.

"Casey," Darius greeted.

I had to swallow again. "I, uh... We're at his house. I found something. Can we talk?"

There was some rustling in the background, and I assumed he was going to a quieter place for privacy.

"Something wrong?" he asked.

You could say that.

"I found photos in his office," I stated. "I'd call them mugshots, but I have a feeling they're all innocent." Mugshot was only fitting because of how the young men and women were posing. Half of them looked drugged. Many were malnourished. Most of them had bruises and cuts all over their bodies. "I think they're trafficking victims. Men and women—all on the young side, maybe older teens, early twenties—beaten up, starved, holding up signs with serial numbers."

I was met with silence.

I couldn't blame him.

Wanting to get it all out as fast as possible, I told him where I'd found the photos, approximately how many there were, that I was using gloves, and that I was currently taking pictures of them to forward to him. And I explained that I wanted to tell him right away in case he had instructions for me, because this went beyond merely casing the joint. This was damning evidence that would—hopefully—put AJ Lange on fucking death row.

Darius cleared his throat. "If they look malnourished in the photos, it's safe to assume their organization starts keeping records once the kids have been held hostage for a while. Maybe there's a hub of sorts in Nevada that they go through before they're sold off or shipped to an auction." He blew out a harsh breath, and I could sense his mind was spinning as quickly as mine was. The difference was, I didn't work in intelligence, and I would be useless at drawing the conclusions he was able to with his training and experience. "I'll have to think about this," he said. "I'm glad you called me, though. It might change our plans a bit. Get ready just in case. Maybe you and Boone will have to go in sooner and clear the house." He paused. "You know what—it's great you're taking pictures. I want you to make them good. No glares or anything—because if the evidence somehow disappears in the next several days, we'll need you to replant it."

I understood. That made sense. There was definitely a risk that these pictures might move to another spot when the whole fucking family showed up, and God knew what they had planned.

"I'll document all of them," I promised.

"Good job. Send them to me later."

Well, yeah, but... "I'll send them to Willow. Unless you've learned how to accept encrypted files that fly under the NSA radar."

"Uh. Send them to Willow."

I cracked a quick smirk. Thought as much.

FOURTEEN

This was it.

I was in love with him. I was in love with us, with everything we shared, with our future.

Every fiber of my being screamed for Ace when we left AJ's house, but we couldn't pick her up right away. I'd completely lost my appetite, so we went straight home and began sorting through our findings. I didn't talk much—which Boone noticed, judging by the looks of concern he fired my way every now and then—but he left me alone while I edited the photos of the trafficking victims.

I'd told him about them. I'd also told him I didn't want him to see them.

It took me three hours to work my way through sixty-two images and make them look like copies of the originals. Sixty-two faces so devoid of hope that I kinda wanted to kill myself near the end.

Whatever Darius had in store for the Langes, I prayed at least some of these innocent boys and girls would find their way home to family, friends, and freedom again. And that the Langes died painfully.

The moment I'd sent the files to Willow, I closed my laptop and fell back against the couch cushions with a heavy sigh. I scrubbed hard at my face, in desperate need to erase the victims from my memory.

"Did you get it done?" Boone asked.

"Yeah," I muttered behind my hands. I let them fall to my sides when I heard him open the window, and I saw he'd made me a drink. Rum and Coke, it looked like.

"I figured you needed one."

He figured right.

"Thanks."

As I straightened in my seat and accepted my drink, he sat down on the edge of the coffee table and pulled out a pack of smokes.

I took one. Hadn't smoked in probably three years, but now was the time. Once upon a time, I'd been a social smoker, Boone more so than me. We'd been social about a whole lot, I guessed. Reckless weekend warriors. Parties that went on for days.

It'd all ended pretty much overnight when Ace landed in our laps.

Ace.

My chest constricted. I wanted to go pick her up soon. I just needed something in between, something that created a gap between trafficking victims and our daughter.

I took a big swig from the glass and let the rum do its job.

"Tell me what to do to make it better." He extended his lighter and lit my smoke, then his own.

I coughed on the first inhale. Christ.

The second was better. Same with the next gulp of my drink.

I gestured toward our makeshift pinboard on the wall where we had a bunch of notes, printouts, images, and lists. I'd seen him add things to it in the past few hours.

"Talk money with me," I requested. "I was kinda out of it after I saw the photos."

I'd still been there. I'd just...gone through the motions. I'd cracked open the safe, which had made me lose more respect for AJ as a criminal, because the lock had been too easy to open without any signs of forced entry. I'd also taken more pictures, but I couldn't for the life of me remember specifics. I'd only managed to snap out of my temporary depression to make sure we didn't leave any traces behind when we left.

"By the way, when did AJ get home?" I asked.

"About two hours after we were gone." He flicked some ashes into an old soda can. "No audio's been picked up yet, though."

Good to know. Whatever audio we got from AJ's house would be recorded and stored in one of my laptops in the closet.

"But okay—money. There'll be a shitload of it." Boone reached behind him and grabbed my camera. "Presuming we won't touch anything that's hard to sell without leaving a trail of evidence—mainly art—we're still looking a lot of green here. Twelve $1500 suits, expensive shoes, thirty-seven one-carat diamonds, about a dozen rare, first-edition books—so far, anyway. I'm still going through his shelves. A rough estimate of twenty K in cash, watches worth at least half a mil, kitchen appliances for about five grand, and...I don't even know about the golf clubs yet. And I still have more photos to look at."

Hot fucking damn. He'd been busy while I'd edited in misery.

Boone flipped through the images on the camera and showed me a couple on the screen. It was AJ's collection of watches.

Jesus. We could go nuts.

It was going to be difficult to leave shit behind. After all, it had to look like he hadn't been robbed to an outsider. So while we wouldn't take the majority of the suits or clean out his kitchen or fill our vehicle with all the golf clubs, we would definitely shop till we dropped.

Seeing dollar signs flash before my eyes did brighten my mood.

I finished my smoke and took the camera, then pinched the screen and zoomed in on some of the watches. I wasn't an expert, but I knew Richard Mille, Jaeger, Rolex, and Piguet. Some of these pieces started at thirty grand.

"You know what this means?" I paused at a picture from the kitchen. Mom would love that juice press. "We can buy a house."

Boone joined me at my side and pressed a kiss to my shoulder. "I was hoping you'd say that."

I smiled a little and took my first easy breath in hours.

"Daddy, you're hugging me a little too hard."

"Am not." I gave her another squeeze before I reluctantly let her go.

Ace snickered at me and returned her attention to the TV.

I shouldn't push it. I was getting exactly what I needed tonight, a movie night with Boone and Ace, all in PJs for the special occasion, under the covers, snacks all around. In our family, pajamas were sacred for Christmas and nights like this one, and it was why we each had two sets. Well, Boone and I. Ace had countless. But on Christmas morning, even Boone and I donned flannel PJs and Santa hats. For movie nights, Boone had his Hulk pajamas, and I had a set with the blue Care Bear printed all over.

Our girl had picked them out for us.

I found ways to look at Ace more than the movie. Not that *Brother Bear* wasn't a masterpiece by Disney, but today had really taken its toll on me. I felt overprotective and needed reassurance that everything was okay. That she was here, free, happy, safe, parked in the middle of the pullout with Boone and me on her flanks.

She laughed at something that happened in the movie and threw a handful of popcorn into her mouth.

"He reminds me of you, Dad!" She giggled at Boone and pointed to the TV, where a big bear did something funny. "He's a goof."

"I'm not a goof." Boone pretended to be offended and reached for two Cheetos that he stuck up his nose. "I'm the most serious person I know!"

I grinned.

Ace didn't know what to do with herself, she was laughing too hard.

"Why are you laughing at me?" he demanded. "Huh?"

"You're so silly!" she guffawed.

I wanted more memories. Grabbing my phone from the table next to the couch, I said, "Lemme take a picture of you."

"Okay!" Ace scooted closer to Boone, and she didn't stop

there. She stuck two Cheetos up her nose too. Then I had the two of them, Ace halfway up on Boone's lap, smiling goofily while I took a photo.

Perfect. My new home screen.

"You look a little serious, but we can't have it all," I said.

Ace peered down her nose and pursed her lips, then breathed out until the Cheetos popped out.

I laughed softly. "They don't go back in the bag."

"Yeah, no. Gross." She deserted the popcorn bowl and crawled over me to drop the snacks on my plate from dinner. The ribs had been delicious once I'd showered off the day and listened to the two clowns engage in a tickle war while preparing for the movie night. And if I got lucky, I'd hear their laughter in my dreams tonight instead.

On the way back to her seat, Ace nearly kneed me in the balls and rubbed her nose against mine.

"Boop!" she chirped.

"Yeah, boop," I chuckled through a grunt. Fuck, close call.

Oblivious to how she'd almost crushed the family jewels, she plopped back on the mattress and declared we needed more popcorn. So I guessed that was my job.

"Comin' right up." I grabbed the bowl and left the bed.

In the kitchen, I dug out the last Jiffy Pop from a cupboard and put it on the stove. It'd been BOGO at Walmart a few weeks ago, so I'd stocked up. Evidently not well enough. Ace had a severe popcorn addiction.

"I'll be right back," I heard Boone say.

"I'll miss you," Ace sang.

I smiled and leaned back against the sink.

Boone appeared in the kitchen doorway a couple seconds later with the remnants of the amusement from Ace's comment in his eyes. Seeing him in higher spirits still gave me the best feeling. In retrospect, I must've been affected by his depressed state for longer than I'd known, because it seemed every smile mattered.

"I need your help with something." He closed the distance between us and landed his hands on the counter behind me, effectively caging me in. I raised a brow in question. "Maybe you can figure this out." He kept his voice down, which intrigued me. It meant he didn't want Ace to hear. "I can't stop thinking about you. Everything you do turns me on or makes me wanna kiss the daylights outta you. I can no longer imagine spending a night without you next to me. I want a future with you—a house, road trips, camping in the desert, fuckin' bake sales, and soccer games."

Well, fuck me. I swallowed a bout of nerves and suddenly understood the concept of butterflies in your stomach. This was what that felt like.

He leaned in and rested his forehead to mine. "I constantly wanna get my arms around you," he murmured. "When you laugh, it automatically makes me feel better."

I smiled unsurely, on the edge of my proverbial seat, and fidgeted with the drawstrings of his PJ bottoms.

"So you tell me, Case," he said quietly. "Think I'm in love?"

A breath gusted out of me in a light laugh, and I shook my head at him. Because of how *Boone* he was. And to me, that was perfection.

"It certainly sounds like it." I cleared my throat and did my best not to respond with just a shit-eating grin.

"It feels like it too."

I swallowed again, then pressed my lips to his and shifted my hands up to his neck. "I'm, uh—I'm good with that. Hella good."

"Yeah?" He smiled into the kiss and gripped my hips.

"Yeah. I told you, I like it when we're on the same page." It was crazy how easy it was to tune out the popcorn popping on the stove once I inched back and got trapped in his affectionate gaze. "You want me to say it, don't you?"

"Damn right." He grazed his teeth along my jaw until he reached my ear. "Let me hear the words, baby."

I shuddered. "I love you. All right? I love you."

He groaned under his breath and kissed me hard, his hands coming up to my neck. He controlled every movement and demanded every bit of my attention with that kiss.

It wasn't until I heard little feet padding closer—too close, too fast—that I broke away. Boone wrenched himself away too, but it was too late. When Ace appeared in the doorway, she came to a screeching halt, and her eyes went wide.

Fuck.

I coughed and scrubbed a hand over my mouth, and Boone backed off as much as he could in the tiny space. Jesus Christ, my ears hadn't felt this hot since I was thirteen and Ma caught me smoking weed in the garage.

"I-I j-just," Ace stammered and pointed to the stove.

Right. The stove. The popcorn was done. I cleared my throat and turned off the heat.

"Sweetie, are you okay?" Boone asked carefully.

She turned her gobsmacked stare to him instead and blinked. Slowly but surely, her cheeks flushed pink, and she went rigid. As if her mind was done confirming what she'd actually seen.

"Yes," she managed to get out. "No. I don't—I-I don't know."

Her breathing picked up quickly. Sensing that she was gonna get upset, I opened my mouth to suggest we sit down and talk, but before I could get a single word out, she bolted down the hall and closed herself into her room.

I suppressed a sigh and hurried after her, Boone close behind me. I'd heard the door slam shut but not the lock being turned. Not that it mattered. We'd raised Ace to respect a closed door, partly because her father and I took on jobs where we *didn't* respect closed doors, and there might be things— evidence, equipment—that we didn't want her to see.

She'd always been equally mindful and curious, and she knew when to stop prodding. We couldn't thank her for that by plowing down the door now.

I knocked instead. "Sweet pea, can you let us in? We'd like to talk to you. It's nothing bad whatsoever. This is a good thing."

"It's a wonderful thing," Boone tacked on. "I think you'll be happy once the surprise settles."

I pinched my lips together and waited for her response, and all I heard was her muffled crying. It shot a ton of worry through me, but I wanted to believe Boone was right. She was just surprised.

"I can't talk right now!" she sobbed. "I'm busy bawling my eyes out!"

I winced and glanced at Boone. "She'll be going through puberty in a few years."

"Don't remind me," he muttered. Then he addressed Ace again. "Can you tell us why you're crying?"

"I don't know why," she wailed. "Are you dying? Am *I* dying?" Her cries got louder, and now she could forget about us staying on this side of the door.

I had fucking limits.

Boone and I entered her room and found her on the bed, crying into her pillow.

"No one's dying, Paisley. Why on earth would you think so?" I carefully sat down on the edge of her bed and placed a hand on her back.

Boone squatted down by her nightstand.

She sniffled around a sob, refusing to come up for air. "When Elliott's parents got divorced, they changed their minds and got back together, and then his mom died of cancer."

Oh Christ.

"Elliott?" Boone mouthed.

"From school," I murmured. "But that's not what's happening here, Ace. Daddy and I were just stupid. We fought so much because we didn't understand that we really liked each other." He owed me a blow job or something for this. In reality, he'd been stupid. I'd been a genius all along—a genius who knew his feelings. "Plus, we grew up as brothers. It made us confused, and it was easier to lash out than talk about it."

Ace whimpered into her pillow. "That sounds so dumb."

That was one way of putting it.

"It can't come as a surprise that we're dumb sometimes," he reasoned.

She sniffled some more, and she finally reemerged from her pillow. Her adorable face was streaked with tears, and her cheeks were red.

I leaned toward her and brushed some hair away from her face. "We've got our shit together now, I promise. All we want is to be a family."

She chewed on her lip and wiped her eyes. "You'll be like boyfriends instead of brothers?"

I looked to Boone and found no support there. He was staring back at me with hesitation and question etched in his forehead, meaning it was up to me to decide how much we divulged to Ace.

This was the girl who'd shoplifted her first candy bar at six, the girl who'd looked at Ma weirdly the time she'd spoken baby talk to Ace—we'd never fucking done that—the girl who called her teachers morons for asking stupid questions, and the girl who loved to tag along when her daddies worked. Last family reunion, she'd taught her uncle Darius that it was okay to steal from Big Corp and the government but never from the "little guy." She'd also asked her uncle Ethan—another cousin of ours, who happened to run a gym—if he could teach her how to throat punch.

She was a chip off the old block, which both terrified me and caused my chest to swell with pride. One day, Boone and I were going to get what was coming to us. The shit we'd pulled on Ma over the years was gonna come back and bite us in the ass, 'cause unlike our mom, we'd trained our daughter.

So I reckoned I had my answer. I didn't need to sugarcoat anything for Ace.

I scooted a little closer and gathered her hands in mine. "We've never been great at following the law," I started out by saying. A bit of an understatement. "So the odds of us giving a fraction of a fuck about society's rules aren't good. Boone and I will always be brothers, but we're, first and foremost, your parents. Parents who happen to love each other very much." I paused and took a lot of relief from the minuscule smile she was trying to hide. "Since we're not actually related, we can be everything to each other."

Ace sniffled and wiped away the last of her tears.

"How does that sound, baby?" Boone asked her.

She withdrew her hands from mine and squirmed in her seat. "Good, maybe? It's gonna be weird at first, I think. You've been fighting so much." She started twisting a lock of hair between her fingers, a telltale sign she was thinking hard. "Are we gonna move?"

I let Boone answer that one.

"Hopefully." He reached out and rubbed her knee over her fabulous *Blossom* PJs. "We need a bigger house, don't we? With a yard and shit."

She was thawing, for sure. "Can we have a pool?"

"Of course!" Boone said it like any other alternative would've been offensive.

"In a few weeks, they'll go on sale everywhere," I added. "We'll need one big enough for Boone."

That earned me a punch in my calf, and that fucking hurt.

"Asshole," I gritted.

"So some things won't change," Ace deadpanned.

No, they wouldn't, and she would find comfort in that, I was certain of it. Because she was a goofball too, and once she saw that my fights with Boone were no longer serious, she'd join in on the fun.

"You feelin' better now, hon?" I grabbed her hand again and kissed her knuckles.

She nodded and smiled. "But it's gonna be *so* weird to see my parents kiss."

I exhaled a laugh and yanked her onto my lap so I could give her a big hug. "I bet it'll be weird to have two parents to make sure you go to bed on time too."

She scrunched her nose at that.

"To answer your question," Boone said, "yes, we will team up against you."

"Oh no!" She giggle-groaned and slapped her hands to her face.

I smiled and kissed the side of her head.

We were gonna be great.

Waking up slowly was my favorite, even more so now when I had Boone in my bed.

It was too early to get up, too early to worry about Ace rising anytime soon, too early for alarm clocks and speaking.

In other words, it was the perfect time to just cuddle and feel each other up.

I pressed a kiss to his neck as he shifted against my morning wood.

The only minor drawback to living with him was that he ran hotter than the devil, so he liked cranking up the AC to the point where I didn't wanna poke a single toe outside the covers. On the flipside, *he ran hotter than the devil*, which turned him into my personal radiator.

He hummed when I found him rock hard and wrapped my fingers around him. Then he shifted against my cock again and made his intentions very clear.

I let out a breath and stroked him unhurriedly, refusing to rush things—for now. I wasn't sure I could be too careful later.

It turned me on so fucking much to control his movements. I knew how to rub his cock to make him tense up, where to brush my fingers to set off a shiver, and how much to tighten my hold to cause him to exhale and groan.

I kissed my way down to the spot between his shoulder blades, and I pressed my cock between his ass cheeks. I wanted him to feel me before I got the lube.

I started stroking him off a little faster.

"Fuck," he breathed.

My mouth watered. Every time I watched the muscles in his back ripple, I wanted to slam my cock into him.

I was done waiting. With another kiss to his warm skin, I released his cock and twisted my body to reach for the lube.

It was so damn liberating to be with him. Not just for the obvious reasons, but for how well we read each other. We didn't need to talk in order to establish trust or set boundaries for certain things. A lifetime together had made us experts at sensing what the other was going through, what the other needed. And right now, his growing impatience was enough. It permeated every movement and every breath.

Once my cock was coated, I shifted closer and pressed

myself between his ass cheeks, and he exhaled and moved with me. My forehead landed in the soft dip between his shoulder blades. He was fucking magnificent, this big beast of a man. With all heart underneath.

I sucked in a breath as the head of my cock breached the tight ring of muscle. Rather than tensing up, Boone groaned under his breath and pushed back against me, forcing my cock deeper into him. Jesus Christ, we were born to be each other's ass sluts.

Desire whipped up a storm within me, making me hungrier and more demanding. He was right. Close wasn't close enough. Closer wasn't enough either. I gripped his hip and slipped my other arm under his neck, and I latched on to him like a fucking leech. With a roll of my pelvis, I buried myself all the way in and slid out again. His breathing grew shallow and rapid, and every inhale and exhale spurred me on.

I knew what kind of fire he was riding on right now. I knew the consuming burn and how the pleasure rolled in slower, inch by inch, fucking with his head, turning him on, making him ravenous.

He tilted his face into the pillow and moaned.

I fucked him a little deeper, a little harder, a little faster.

I heard the slick sounds from us. Both from working my cock in and out of him and his hand stroking his cock. I felt the muscles in his arm ripple, same with the muscles in his back.

The pain was fading for him.

I caught his neck in the crease of my arm and reached down to touch his chest, brushing my fingers through his chest hair. I pinched his nipple lightly and abandoned his hip for his cock. I wanted to feel him pulse in my hand. He trembled as I took over, clenching and relaxing, clenching and relaxing.

His cock was wet with pre-come, and I rubbed it in with firm strokes and cupped my hand over the blunt head.

He started panting. For a moment, I didn't even have to move. He pushed into my hand, then back on my cock, chasing every sensation I gave him.

The buildup was too brief. I went from wanting to prolong this for hours to needing to get off in mere seconds.

"Boone," I croaked, out of breath.

"I'm so fucking close," he gasped, reaching for something. Whatever it was, he slipped it under him, near his cock. Maybe his boxers—I didn't fucking care. "Fuck me, little brother. Fuck me hard."

I screwed my eyes shut and groaned against his shoulder. Then I let my body take over completely, and I chased my orgasm in hard thrusts that slapped my pelvis against his ass. Every time I buried my cock all the way in, I was overcome with pleasure. He was so goddamn warm, tight, and wet. Wet with lube, wet with come.

He pushed off the covers and rocked into my hand, and he went rigid all over. My body was sufficiently overheated that the chill blasting us only felt good.

His orgasm set off mine. I felt his hot release shoot between my fingers, and I just barely managed to tighten my grip on him and stroke him faster before I surrendered to my climax.

Holy fuck.

My heart thundered.

I fucked rope after rope of come deep into his ass.

He clamped down on me.

Sex had never been so motherfucking good.

A steady current of shivers flowed through us, and for several beats, all I heard were our shallow breaths.

I swallowed against the dryness in my throat.

"Jesus Christ," he rasped. He moved something made of fabric over my hand, and I cracked one eye open and lifted my heavy head to look. It was his boxers. Good thinking. Now we didn't have to get up to change the sheets. "My ass feels raw," he murmured hoarsely. "How long does it take to recover?"

I exhaled a laugh and carefully withdrew from him.

He winced. "I'm serious. From now on, one of us is getting fucked every night."

I smiled and yawned and rolled onto my back to stretch out. "We can flip-fuck each other until we can't walk."

"What's a flip-fuck? You have a lot to teach me." He discarded his boxers, then returned his heat to me and landed his head on my chest. "But for the sake of my sanity, we're gonna pretend you learned everything from the internet."

I chuckled. "Flip-fuck just means we take turns."

He hummed and kissed my chest. "Which you learned from the internet. Right?"

"Right." I couldn't kill the grin on my mug. Fuck, how I loved him.

FIFTEEN

I'd waited long enough. It was time to reintroduce some old traditions.

Maybe we could bring Ace. Make it a family thing. Or—actually, no. There would be countless family things, but sometimes, I wanted Case to myself.

I picked up the phone and dialed the number I'd found online.

"You've reached Giordano's. This is Zoe speaking. How may I help you?"

"I'd like to make a reservation," I said.

For our first official date—at our place.

Our early Monday morning in bed was the last peaceful moment we got that week. Boone and I threw ourselves back into work, and it was basically the only thing we did while Ace was in school. We kept going through the photos from AJ's house, mapping out his life and personality as best as we could, we replayed the audio from his office whenever his car was parked at home, and we sent all our theories and information to Willow.

The man was insanely careful. Even when we got him on tape, he didn't say anything incriminating. There were a few dates and locations mentioned, leads for Darius and his crew to follow up on, but nothing that made us jump out of our seats.

On Wednesday, we dropped off Ace for dinner at Mom's place so Boone could check out the old brothel outside of town and I could break in to the hospitality guy's apartment.

Oliver Hansen led a modest life, despite that he probably earned well enough at the Venetian. His apartment was in a nice complex near Downtown Summerlin, but the security was downright crap. I was in and out of his two-bedroom apartment in under an hour, and I didn't exactly leave empty-handed.

I'd transferred a total of forty gigabytes of documents from his home computer, I'd gotten my hands on approximately seventeen passwords that Oliver kept on a damn note in his desk, I'd taken photos of anything interesting in his place, and a handful of $100 poker chips had somehow jumped down into my pockets.

On my way back to Ma's place, I called Boone and found out he was on his way back too. I stalled by stopping at a Chevron for gas and a six-pack of Mom's favorite beer. We hadn't told Ace not to say anything about Boone and me being together—on purpose—so chances were, we'd need to butter Mom up a bit. At the register, I decided to get her some scratch-offs too. She loved those.

Boone was already parked outside Ma's house when I pulled up, and I smirked when he stepped out of his truck.

I killed the engine but stayed in my seat to replace my black hoodie with my favorite denim shirt. "You afraid to face Mom without me?"

"We threw our daughter to the wolves unprepared, in hopes she'd talk, so I don't think I'm the only one nervous right now."

He had a point.

I folded the sleeves past my elbows and then ran a hand through my hair and checked the rearview. No need to look like I'd just committed a crime.

"How did it go out there, by the way?" I asked.

Boone shrugged and cracked his knuckles absently. "It almost feels like a dead lead. We can't find the new owner—if there is one—or link it to the Langes. And the site itself is a dump."

Hmm. "What needs to be done out there? Like, if the Langes are planning to use the site for something when they arrive, can they?"

"Fuck no. We're talking total renovations. The building is standing, but that's about it. I peered inside, and it's in complete shambles. At least two walls have met a sledgehammer, the stairs to the second floor are missing steps, there're trash bags in the corners, a hole in the lobby area's floor, and a couple windows are cracked. I took photos—you can see for yourself later."

Part of me wanted to solve the puzzle, but a bigger part of me was ready to put all this behind me. We'd done our job. All we had left was to continue to provide Willow and Darius with the intel that ran through the channels we'd opened. Allegra was gonna give me a new report tomorrow, we had around-the-clock surveillance on AJ, we were about to map out Oliver Hansen's work with the Langes, and we'd created a library of pictures that would help our cousins profile their targets.

I was ready for payday.

"I guess it doesn't matter anymore," I said, leaving my car. "We've done what we were supposed to do—and then some. I'll send everything to Willow and update her whenever we find out something new, but otherwise..." I shrugged. "All we gotta do is wait for Darius's call."

Boone nodded with a dip of his chin. "It'll be nice seeing him this week."

Absolutely. He was driving here from Washington on Thursday—just him and his kids—with everyone else following this weekend. I didn't know exactly how big their crew would be, but it sounded like several people would be involved.

The sound of a door opening had my attention, and just as I turned around, I heard Mom's voice.

"You boys gonna stand there all day, or will you come inside and explain to me why Ace tells me her daddies are getting married?"

Welp.

Nerves tightened my gut, and I quickly snatched up the six-pack of beer from the back seat. Then I exchanged a brief, panicked look with my brother and dug out the scratch-off tickets from my back pocket.

"Here goes everything," he muttered. "What if she doesn't approve?"

That kinda calmed me down. She was our mother, for fuck's sake. Of course she was gonna approve.

"She has to," I replied firmly. "We're her angels."

Boone offered a dubious look and nothing else.

With the beer and scratch-offs in my arms, I took the lead and walked up the path to her house. "Hey, Ma. You look extra beautiful today."

"Oh, cut the shit." She had no problems accepting my gifts, but the ice in her tone would require more than that in order to melt. "Let's talk in the living room."

Fuck.

With those words, combined with the sound of Boone shutting the door behind us, I felt thirteen again. Even in our midthirties, we could shrink under Ma's stare. Probably because she had the patience of a saint and rarely got really pissed.

Ace was waiting for us in the living room, and she jumped up at the sight of us. "Dads! I didn't know I wasn't supposed to say anything."

"You did nothing wrong, hon," I said quickly. That was the last thing I wanted her to believe. "Boone and I just figured Gramma would never be mad at *you*, so it was better if you let something slip before we got here. Kinda like cushioning the blow."

She blinked and plopped down in the middle of the couch again.

"Are you freaking kidding me?" Ma exclaimed. "You threw your own daughter under the bus?"

No! Sort of!

"We didn't throw her," Boone replied defensively. "We very gently placed her under the tires."

"Also," I added quickly, "if you refer to yourself as a big bus in this scenario, you might suffer from internalized misogyny. You should work on that."

Mom did a double take at me, eyes filled with disbelief, before she pinched the bridge of her nose and pointed at the couch. "Sit the fuck down."

Boone and I sat the fuck down.

I swallowed hard as Mom started pacing on the other side of the coffee table.

Ace glanced up at me, then at Boone. "You're kinda roofless, Daddy."

Boone's forehead creased.

"Ruthless," I supplied.

"That's what I said!" Ace snapped.

I nodded. Bad time to disagree with the women in our family. Bad, bad time.

"Let me get this straight, Casey." Mom came to a stop and faced us dead-on. "The time I watched Paisley at the Venetian, you returned drunk—in the middle of the night—and slurred about Boone kissing you. Did that actually happen?"

I'd done what?

I widened my eyes and tried to search through my memories. But honest to God, that night was kinda fuzzy. I remembered we had a good time. I remembered going to a bar, then a club, and there was no forgetting the fantastic make-out session. But exactly what I'd told Ma when we got back to the hotel room was asking a bit much.

Apparently, Boone recalled. "Yeah, that happened." He looked too somber for my liking. It raised my hackles—I couldn't fucking help it—because Boone was supposed to be happy and carefree. "I don't know word for word what Ace told you, but Case and I are together. I love him."

As if I could stop myself from smiling at him now.

"I told her you're getting married," Ace said frankly.

"We don't know that, sweet pea," I cautioned her. "Marriage isn't on our radar." I flicked a glance at Ma and said, "There hasn't been a proposal or anything. We haven't even discussed it."

"You don't honestly think marriage is the issue here, do you?" she grated, annoyed.

Well, fuck. No, maybe not.

"My bad. I'm just sayin'." Time to circle back to what Boone had said. "What Boone confirmed is true, though. And I love him too."

Mom was still upset. She folded her arms over her chest and stared at the ground. "I fuckin' hate this. I want y'all to be happy, but sweet baby Jesus, you boys are always kicking curve balls straight into my face. I'm your *mother*. And now you might force me to accept that one of you is no longer my child? I can't do that."

I furrowed my brow, confused as shit. "Wait, what? Why would—"

"Well, I don't know the goddamn law on this, Casey!" she cried out. "Are you even allowed to have a relationship if you're both legally my sons?"

A big breath gusted out of Boone, and his shoulders sagged. It looked like it was relief rolling off him, though that seemed too soon for me.

"*That's* what you're worried about?" he asked. "Mom— Christ—who gives a shit about a piece of paper? We haven't looked into things either, but it doesn't fucking matter. Case will always be your son, irregardless of what happens in official records."

I grimaced. "Irregardless ain't a word."

"Focus, or I swear to God!" he yelled at me.

Both Ace and I jumped in our seats, and she crawled up in my lap.

The regret in Boone's expression was instant.

"Don't be scared, sweetheart." I hugged her and kissed her hair. "He wasn't yelling at you, you know that."

"I'm not scared," she whispered in my ear. "I'm gonna use it against him to get a cat."

I pressed my lips together in a tight line.

Man, I loved this girl. She had potential. *Brilliant* mind, though she needed to learn that in a quiet room, even whispers were heard by those nearby.

At least Boone calmed down. He groaned a chuckle and scrubbed his hands over his face.

I scooted closer to him and told Ace to give Daddy a hug. It looked like he needed it.

"You can chill now, Daddy." She wrapped her arms around his neck and patted him on the head.

It was a sweet sight. I smiled to myself as Boone deflated and hugged her back.

When I glanced over at Mom again, I saw that the fight had left her too. The worry lines in her forehead were in full effect and her eyes were brimming with tears, but the anger had evaporated.

I walked over to her and squeezed her to me. "No one can take our relationship away from us, Ma. I swear to you, I'll always be one of the two sons who give you grief."

She laughed tearfully and smacked my arm lightly. "Grief and gray hairs."

"That's what's up." I smiled down at her and hoped everything was okay.

She could probably read my mind. "We'll be fine, sugar." She reached up and patted my cheek. "It threw me for a moment."

I nodded. "I guess we're good at that."

"World champions," she agreed. "One thing's for sure. I'll never be bored."

I chuckled.

Yeah. We'd definitely be fine.

I didn't know who was the most excited to see Darius that Thursday, Ace or me. Boone loved the man too, but he'd always been closer to Ryan and Jake, and Jake wasn't with us anymore. He'd died in Afghanistan years ago.

Someone stepped out on the patio, and I looked over my shoulder to see Boone with a big platter of meat. Steaks, chicken, hot dogs, burger patties.

"Darius likes his steak rare," I reminded him.

"I remember, you fuckin' fanboy." He shook his head in amusement and set the meat next to the grill. A new grill. We'd picked it up at Walmart today. Half-off, because some asshole had dented the lid.

The nerve of some people.

Music poured out from the living room, and I would've fist-bumped Mom if she'd been out here. She'd put on Cyndi Lauper. It was a mix CD I'd made her, so I knew it went "True Colors" and then "Girls Just Want to Have Fun." While I was hooked on the '90s, Ma was addicted to the '70s, but we met in the middle and loved '80s music together.

She came out next and set a stack of plates in front of me, followed by silverware and napkins.

"You sure you don't want me to help?" I asked. For the second time. Boone had called dibs on the grill, which evidently meant there was nothing else for me to do.

"No, you just sit there, sugar. I don't want you ruining the side dishes." She patted my head on the way back in again. Thanks a lot for the vote of confidence. "You can set the table and fold the napkins!" she hollered in afterthought.

"I guess it's because you're a really craptastic cook," Ace mentioned casually.

I frowned at her and started setting out the plates. "The fuck you saying? You've never complained before."

She rolled her eyes and grabbed the napkins. "Heating frozen pizza and popping English muffins in the toaster isn't the same as cooking, Dad. You're *great* at heating up what machines made in a factory."

Technically, I knew that was criticism, but she'd also called me great at doing what I was already doing.

Boone found her funny. "Don't hold back, baby G."

Ace scrunched her nose. "You're hardly better."

"Oh-ho!" I laughed.

Finding no support from our girl, Boone turned around and focused on the grill instead. Ace and I moved on too, and we decided to warm up for the barbecue by doing our best Darius impressions.

"Do the one from Easter last year," I requested. "When he got so mad."

Ace giggled and repositioned herself in the chair so she sat on her knees. And she puffed out her chest and tried to look all grumpy and stern. She was too fucking cute.

"That's why you can't trust the government," she kinda... growl-scoff-mocked. "You know they're just gonna grease one another's pockets and grumble-grumble-grumble. It ain't like they'll get caught, grumble-grumble. It's them against the people."

I laughed and shook my head.

Boone left the grill and sat down across from us, which was when I realized he had a beer and I didn't. What the hell?

"Your turn," he told me. "Do Darius when he's had a few."

"Oooh, that's a funny one!" Ace all but bounced in her seat.

I cleared my throat and took a deep breath, summoning my inner Ron Swanson. 'Cause that's exactly who Darius was. This grouchy, forty-four going on eighty-four, misanthropic libertarian who claimed to hate everyone when, in reality, he'd die and kill for those he loved—and others. After all, he'd spent his life rescuing people.

"All right, all right, just hear me out," I slurred. "Listen to what I have to say. Hear me out. Look—do I hate mankind? Yeah. But do I think they're irredeemable? Well yeah, that too." At that, Ace cracked up, and I used it. I grabbed her shoulder and swayed a little when I spoke. "Quit laughin' at me. Hear me out—hear me out! Y'all just don't listen to me. But one day, you'll fuckin' see. I'm right. I'm always right."

Ace giggled madly behind her hands, her cheeks flushed, and Boone merely grinned at me.

Truth be told, I was expecting laughter. My impression was spot-on!

Then I felt the slightest breeze brush against my neck, and my body reacted as if a hurricane had just wrecking-balled its way through Nevada. I tensed up in my seat, warning bells went off, and I stared at Boone just as he flicked a glance somewhere behind me.

Fuck.

I swallowed. "He's behind me, isn't he?"

Boone's grin widened, and he took a swig of his beer.

Shit, shit, shit.

"Heh." I shifted in my seat to peer behind me, and sure enough, I was fucked. Mom and Darius stood in the doorway, Darius with an unreadable expression—which was his forte—one kid on his hip and another plastered to his side. "Hey, Darius. Long time, no see."

Jayden, the eldest boy, looked to be around Ace's age, and he was smirking a little. He stuck to Darius but didn't strike me as shy, unlike the younger boy. Justin. He was about four and presumably autistic, according to Ma. He had noise-canceling headphones on.

"Let me know when the Casey impressions begin," Darius

drawled, walking farther out on the patio. "All I gotta do is cram a Pop-Tart in my mouth and mimic the vernacular of a '90s Valley girl."

"Oh!" What the fuck! I shot up from my seat. "That's a big word for the Chuck Norris of Washington."

He let out a laugh. "Being called Chuck Norris ain't an insult."

I scoffed and gnashed my teeth. I wanted to be a good host and not scare the youngest boy, so I put a lid on my box of stellar comebacks. "You know what? I won't resort to childish games. That's beneath me."

That made pretty much everyone laugh.

Assholes, all of them.

Darius grinned and extended his hand. "Good to see you, kid."

Yeah, yeah. "You too," I grumbled and shook his hand.

Mom took over from there, running introductions of everyone at the same time as she ordered Boone and me to move out the table so everyone would have room to sit. Ace got to hug her "wicked cool" Uncle Darius, who had changed a lot from last year. He'd always had a spare moment for Ace, but having kids of his own now had softened him a bit. The two boys—and possibly the guy he was with—had smoothed some of the harder edges. It was nice.

While I grabbed an extra chair from the shed, Boone deemed the grill ready and began putting burgers and hot dogs on there.

I noticed Jayden eyeing the community pool nearby, and I encouraged Ace to show the boy around.

"Stay where we can see you," I said.

Jayden flicked a quick glance at Darius, who gave him a nod and sat down with Justin on his lap. Then the two eldest kids were gone, and I asked Mom if she wanted help bringing shit out.

"No, no. You catch up with Darius." She couldn't help herself; she had to hug the man again. "It's so good to have you here, honey. How are all your brothers and sisters?"

"Busting my chops as always." He smiled.

Mom laughed and gave his shoulder an "oh, you" swat before returning inside.

"So you're renting a house in Henderson?" I asked. "That's what Willow mentioned."

Darius inclined his head. "I'll keep the boys with me till the others arrive, and then your ma will take over."

Yeah, Mom already had plans for them.

"I take it Boone and I are on a need-to-know basis?" I had to admit, I was curious about the size of this operation.

"Unless you wanna join in," he replied with a wry smirk.

I chuckled and showed my palms. "You know, I'm good. It's been one hell of a month already."

"Hear, hear," Boone said.

"It's for the best," Darius agreed. "Y'all have done enough." He paused. "Willow sends her gratitude. You've made her work a lot easier. I swear, every time she received a message from you, she got excited."

That was good enough for me. That, and whatever we would get our hands on in AJ's house.

"Anytime." I meant that. This job had been fun. "I gotta ask, though. Who funds you guys? Whatever you're gonna do can't be cheap."

He shrugged and peered down at Justin. The boy was visibly tired and more focused on fiddling with the buttons on Darius's open shirt. The tee he wore underneath was from his restaurant. Quinn's Fish Camp.

"Partly savings," he answered absently. "An old friend is funding too."

Either way, they were paying for this themselves? That was insane.

"Then we'll split the profit," I decided. "Trust, there'll be plenty."

But Darius shook his head. "I appreciate it, but we're not doing this for money. We just wanna wash our hands of everything once it's over."

I hummed. I wouldn't push it—for now.

Mom came out with beers, juice boxes, and condiments, and she said she was ready to put the fries in the fryer. The garlic bread needed another five minutes in the oven.

"Are you double-frying them?" Darius asked.

Mom patted his cheek. "Of course I am. I wouldn't forget your favorite, dear."

Darius grinned. "It's good to be back in Vegas."

It was good to have him here. We usually had our reunions in their neck of the woods—literally, trees fuckin' everywhere—so it'd been a while since they were in Vegas.

Once Mom was out of earshot again, I asked my last question.

"So what do you want from us while y'all are here? Do we just wait by the phone?"

"Pretty much," he said with a nod. "You've already done a great job, Casey. Stand by and wait. Have the photocopies ready just in case." He didn't need to remind me of those. "Be ready on a couple minutes' notice. I can't guarantee you'll have a lot of time to prepare, so pack whatever you need beforehand."

"No problem." We could keep everything we needed in Boone's truck. I twisted the caps off two beers and handed him one. "To family, then. May you and your crew crush the enemy like bugs."

"I'll drink to that." He clinked his bottle to mine before taking a swig. "So what's this shit I heard from Ma about you two shacking up as a couple? When I called you a few weeks ago, you weren't even on speaking terms."

I exchanged a smirk with Boone. "This job happened, I guess."

SIXTEEN

Case knocked on the bathroom door. "Bro. It's been half an hour. That's how you get hemorrhoids."

"Almost done," I murmured absently, scrolling on my phone.

Living in a small trailer with a brother who had complete control of our technology and thought the cops would burst in at the most insignificant Google search had resulted in me sitting here. Secret research on my phone while I was on the shitter. Thank fuck our job was almost over and Case could let go of his paranoia soon.

Although, I kinda wanted to keep this secret a while longer.

So I kept scrolling the local real estate listings. I wanted to get prepared. I wanted to see what was out there and start planning for how I could give Case a home he'd love. Starting with property close to nature. He didn't belong smack-dab in the middle of town, even though I knew he wanted to remain somewhat close. But I knew my brother. He needed peace and quiet more than a bustling nightlife.

He needed a place where he could shut out the world, and it was exactly what I craved too.

"You have two hours, starting right now." Darius's voice was strained and rough, and it shot adrenaline straight through me. "Clean him out—I don't care—but the Feds will show up as soon as you're outta there, and it can't look like he's been robbed. Bring the photocopies and remove the transmitter!" He hung up the phone without another word, and I yanked the cord to the toaster out of the outlet before my Pop-Tarts were ready. Quicker than arguing with a button that didn't always obey me.

"Boone!" I yelled, setting a timer on my phone. "It's go-time!"

What a goddamn week this had been. A week and some changes, even.

For the next couple minutes, Boone and I stumbled around the trailer as we changed clothes, put on the too-big shoes, and gathered our gear. Then we stormed out of there and aimed for his truck. It'd been parked right outside our home for days, just waiting for this moment.

So had my mix CD that I'd prepared.

The glare Boone gave me when he turned the ignition and the music started blaring was quite fucking impressive.

I just felt we needed something that gave us energy, and Vengaboys's "Boom, Boom, Boom, Boom!!" was a great candidate.

"Are you for real?" he snapped over the music.

"I love you too!" I hollered.

He rolled his eyes and tore outta there.

I bobbed my head to the beat and patted my side pockets, making sure I had everything. Few things had been accomplished this week, aside from providing Willow with minor updates, but we'd managed to secure an easier entrance to AJ's estate this time. In exchange for a thousand bucks, Boone's buddy Jay had divulged the passcode to shut off the alarm. Because suddenly we could spend that kind of money and didn't have to rely on others to do the job.

"Did you attach the fake plates?" he asked.

"You know I did." I nodded. It was only a precaution. Fake license plates and a whole lot of dirt on the truck. We'd taken it out for a spin in the desert when we'd burned the evidence of everything we'd been up to this past month. Now the truck looked like it'd just spent a decade in the wilderness. Mud and dust—mostly dust—covered the sides, back, and front. To be honest, I wasn't sure the fake plates were even visible.

We made our way across town and toward Summerlin, and I got ready on the way. We would have the cover of darkness to shield us this time around, so I wasn't even nervous.

We ended up repeating every step. We parked near the cul-de-sac on AJ's street, we put on gloves, we brought our gear, we went around the back and up along the edge of the infinity pool, and—that's where it stopped. Because I finally got to do what an open window prevented me from doing last time. I got to break in to the double-cylinder deadbolt on AJ's terrace.

It took me twenty minutes, but it was worth it.

As soon as the alarm was disconnected, Boone retrieved two

empty duffels from my backpack. We had more in his bag if needed.

"Let's shop."

"Fuck yeah." High on adrenaline and excitement, I yanked him in for a quick, hard kiss.

It left him with that dopey grin I was so fucking in love with.

"You start down here. I'll head upstairs." I checked the timer on my phone. "We have forty-five minutes." It would give us a fifteen-minute window to put as much distance between ourselves and this place before the pigs arrived.

First order of business, I removed the transmitter from the chair in AJ's study, and then I opened the bottom drawer in his desk and checked if the pictures of trafficking victims were still there.

They weren't. How goddamn convenient for AJ. But the sick motherfucker wouldn't get away that easily. I planted the photocopies to replace the missing pictures before closing the drawer again.

"Now. Finally." I opened the other drawers and quickly pocketed all the crumpled bills I could find. How I'd waited for this moment.

The rare, first-edition books on the shelves behind me weren't at the top of the list of priorities, so I went to AJ's bedroom next. Or, to be precise, his walk-in closet.

I came to an abrupt stop in the doorway when I spotted the wall safe. It was fucking open. There were also two briefcases below the safe, and I got the sneaking suspicion that someone had been in a hurry.

I flicked on the light and went down on one knee. The locks on the briefcases just needed some brute force, so I let out a sharp whistle. Boone could handle those. Instead, I straightened again and opened the wall safe farther.

"Fuck me sideways," I mumbled. Three shelves were full of

cash bundles, velvet pouches, poker chips, and binders. It took me ten seconds to get bored with the binders. I was sure AJ's stocks and bonds were worth a shitload, but it was nothing I could get my hands on.

How the hell did I decide what should be left behind? Make sure no one could tell the place had been robbed was the rule. The binders were staying, obviously. But opening one of the velvet pouches, I asked myself, how many diamonds had to stay here?

Boone joined me, a little winded, and asked what was up.

"Well, there've been additions since last time." I gestured to the briefcases and held up a couple pouches.

He got started right away and used a crowbar to open the briefcases.

The first popped open with a strained thud, and my eyes bugged out.

"Jesus," Boone whispered.

He opened the second too.

"Holy fuck, I'm gonna shit myself," I breathed. There had to be two million dollars there. I squatted down and flipped through one cash bundle. All hundred-dollar bills.

"If you tell me we gotta leave this behind, I will shoot your balls off, and I'm a fan of those," he told me.

"Fuck no! We're bringing them both." I opened my duffel and stacked the briefcases inside. "Let's hurry. We can scream like girls at a Backstreet Boys concert when we're outta here."

"I just might, bro."

"I can guarantee I will." I almost wanted to fan my face. I felt a little sweaty. My heart pounded so fast that it was more like an incessant whooshing sound. "Okay, so we'll leave a handful of cash bundles and one pouch of diamonds. Maybe some poker chips too."

He nodded firmly, moving on to the watch collection while I

emptied the safe. The watches were laid out on a lit-up display that ejected from under the rack where AJ kept his ties.

"Do we take 'em all?" he asked.

"Take the most valuable ones," I replied. "Leave a third."

I chewed on my lip, thinking. The cash and diamonds—even the poker chips—wouldn't be an issue at all. The watches, however... The investigators would eventually run across receipts or insurance papers for those. That was how valuable some of the pieces were. But what could they do about it? And hell, for all we knew, AJ had come across them illegally too. We didn't know. And I couldn't imagine that the Feds would spend manpower on dead ends about expensive watches when they were drowning in cases of missing persons and the collapse of a human trafficking ring.

"How much time is left?" Boone asked.

I checked my phone. "Twenty-four minutes. I'll go check the guest rooms."

I didn't expect much in there, but I did get one nice surprise. AJ's mother had been staying here, and the small jewelry case she'd left in the guest bathroom was packed with goodies. I bagged an amethyst-and-diamond necklace, several pairs of earrings, two diamond bracelets, rings with rubies, emeralds, and sapphires, and a couple brooches. Rose gold, yellow gold, white gold, this woman wasn't fucking around with gaudy bling.

When all was said and done, Boone and I walked out of AJ's estate with four heavy duffel bags—and the two backpacks on our backs—and we didn't say a word. Tension had flooded us the moment I'd reactivated the alarm and relocked the patio door. Stiff as boards, we stalked toward the edge of the backyard, where I crossed the pool corner first. Then he slung the bags my way, and I dropped them carefully on the ground below.

It wasn't over until the fat lady sang and all that.

I knew we were thinking the same things. What if we got caught now, with one foot on the finish line? What if we'd forgotten something in the house that would lead the authorities to us? What if, what if, what if?

It took a while for ghosts like that to shut up.

We hadn't forgotten anything. We'd double-checked and triple-checked. Our DNA couldn't be found in that house. Or our fingerprints. We were always careful. They wouldn't even find our correct shoe sizes.

After leaving the duffels and our backpacks in the back seat, we got in and kept an eye on our surroundings. No one lurking. It was a quiet neighborhood. No alarms triggered. No traces. Darius was dealing with AJ's car, or namely, the tracker. I swallowed past the dryness in my throat as Boone pulled away from the curb.

Had we actually pulled it off?

"Why am I surprised that we nailed this?" I asked, baffled. "We're not new. We've been doing this for fifteen years."

"I was just thinking the same," he admitted. "I guess the size of the loot matters."

True. We usually worked with others too. Smaller gigs, smaller rewards, more people.

It made me think of the envelopes we were gonna hand out. It was easy to get greedy and selfish in our business, and that was how one lost connections and friends. We were gonna show our appreciation to Jay, Allegra, Mom, Laney, and a few others.

On that note... "Don't get too attached to the cash in the briefcases. I have plans for us."

It wasn't a new plan. It was something I'd considered for years. Like, "If I ever end up with a lot of money, I wanna find a way to do this and this." And now, we might get that chance. With a bit of luck, Darius could help us.

"I'm not even gonna ask," Boone chuckled. "I'm just relieved right now."

I exhaled and nodded slowly. It was a damn good feeling.

Two days later, I drove down to Henderson with two duffels full of money.

Boone was at Ma's place, along with Ace, Jayden, and Justin. The two boys had apparently taken a liking to Mom, and who could blame them? From my understanding, the boys had spent the whole week at Mom's place, though Darius and his partner Gray had stopped by every day to check in and have dinner or coffee.

I parked outside a nondescript one-story stucco house on a quiet street. Darius had agreed to meet with me before he picked up the kids and started their journey back to Washington.

Maybe Boone and I would live in a house like this soon.

On the other hand, they were kinda dull. So much beige. My family and I weren't meant for a cookie-cutter lifestyle.

In fact, the more I thought about the house, the more I hated it.

I knocked on the door and spied Darius through the living room window. He was closing a black garbage bag. Dressed in a pair of well-worn jeans and a wifebeater, it was easy to see where he'd been injured. One of his knees was wrapped in a bandage. It looked thicker under his jeans. A big wrap poked out from his shoulder blade too when he turned to pick up his flannel from the back of a chair. Too late to cover up, cousin.

He was shrugging the shirt on when he opened the door for me.

"Oi, kid."

I furrowed my brow. "You okay?"

He had minor bruising along his neck and some cuts and scrapes on his arms too.

"I'm fantastic." He opened the door wider and left the hallway. "Coffee? Beer? Coke?"

"Coffee sounds good," I replied, closing the door behind myself.

"In this goddamn heat? You're nuts."

I chuckled and followed him. "You shoulda been here a couple weeks ago. It was brutal."

If I didn't know any better, I'd say they'd hosted one hell of a party here. I passed six big trash bags with takeout containers and pizza boxes trying to poke through the plastic.

"I distinctly remember you saying you hate takeout food," I commented. "I remember because it was the moment you broke my heart."

He let out a gruff laugh and nodded at the patio. He had coffee for me, soda for himself, and a bag of chips.

We sat down on the patio that overlooked a small pool. It was a perfectly nice, middle-class neighborhood, yet the idea of living like this made my skin crawl. It felt almost claustrophobic.

"Do I wanna know what's in those bags?" Darius asked.

I took a breath, unable to shake the unease from being here. It was this place. Freshly mowed lawn, no weeds between the stone tiles, no cracks or dents, no color, no room for flaws.

"Um. Yeah. I mean..." I shook my head and cleared the thoughts. "It's money."

"I figured." He sat forward, observing me, forehead creased, and cracked his knuckles. "What's up, Casey? You look... I don't know."

I had to say something. "Could you imagine living in a

house like this? Minute I sat down, it felt like someone tied a noose around my neck."

A slight smirk tugged at his mouth, and he sat back again and dug out a pack of smokes. "I wouldn't live here for all the money in the world."

It was a relief just to hear him say that.

"I used to picture myself in a small house over by Calico Ridge, Lake Las Vegas—those parts," I mused. "It's gorgeous up there. Especially if you find property on the fringes. Step out on your terrace, and it's all mountains." I gestured with my hands, painting a panorama of the mountain range not far from here. "More greenery too, thanks to the lake." Yeah, that's what I wanted. "Ace wants a pool too—and probably not the above-ground versions I've been eyeing at Sam's."

Darius chuckled and took a drag from his smoke.

"And I want an Airstream in my backyard," I said. "A small silver bullet in the corner—as the barbecue area. You know? Like you see in movies. Firepit, bistro lights, wind chimes, colorful blankets, and whatnot."

He smiled and cocked his head at me. "You lost me at wind chimes, but the rest sounds like a nice goal."

More like a dream. "It's expensive out there." I leaned back in my chair and eyed the yard. "At least along the outer rim. You pay for the view."

He hummed. "Something tells me money won't be an issue anymore."

The memory of standing by our pullout bed at home with all the valuables we'd stolen flashed in my head, and I opened my mouth, only to shut it and rethink my response. Because he'd given me the golden opportunity to broach the topic of why I was here.

"That's why I wanted to talk to you," I admitted. "We scored a fuckload that night—more than we could've hoped for.

And that's before including this." I grabbed the duffels from the ground and placed them on the table. "It's two-point-two mil in cash."

Darius stared at the bags and raked his teeth along his lip.

"Two briefcases full," I said. "This isn't counting the cash we found in the safe." Which was almost thirty grand.

"I had a feeling you'd find more money," he replied. "I'm a *little* surprised you told me about it..."

What the fuck? If he hadn't been smirking to show he was kidding—partly, anyway—I would've been offended.

"I'm ignoring that, you dick." I folded my arms over my chest. "Why did you think we were gonna find more?"

"Because with human trafficking comes a buyer or several," he responded coolly. "We knew there'd been...transactions."

I flinched. I didn't feel bad whatsoever for using money from criminals, but I hoped said criminals were buried in the desert.

"Can I ask?" I wondered.

No, I couldn't.

He shook his head. "All you need to know is I'm satisfied with the outcome, and I don't settle very easily."

That did bring me comfort. It was interesting, though, that we hadn't heard anything on the news yet.

"So what about the money?" he asked. "It's yours."

"It doesn't have to be," I replied bluntly. "I'm not gonna lie, I didn't come here for entirely selfless reasons, but I still saw those photos, Darius. I see their faces every fucking night in my sleep. And knowing y'all were out here, hopefully putting those sick sons'a bitches away, without getting a dime for it...? It doesn't sit well with me."

He said nothing in response; he just looked at me, waiting me out, and it caused more memories to rush back. This was his shtick. The quieter he was, the more others talked. Highly frustrating, highly effective.

"I'm willing to let go of 70% of what's in these bags," I went on. I got a reaction to that. His brows hiked up a bit. He hadn't seen that coming. "You didn't work alone—share it with everyone who helped you. Even if you wanna wash your hands of everything, not everyone has gold buried on their property like you do."

He narrowed his eyes at me. "I don't know what you're talking about."

Oh, sure he didn't. I wasn't born yesterday. I'd seen pictures of his new place up in the woods. More than that, I'd grown up with him. He probably didn't have a savings account, but I'd bet my bottom dollar one would find themselves staring into the barrel of his shotgun if they turned the wrong stone in his yard. Or looked under the mattress.

He moved forward before I could ignore another retort. "You said you weren't here for entirely selfless reasons."

I inclined my head and shifted in my seat. "I need a favor."

"I'm listening."

Here goes.

I took a breath and hoped for the best. "You take 70% of that money, and you hire me at your restaurant. Make up a position. Maybe I'll be a scout of some sort—someone who keeps you updated on the latest culinary trends from Vegas. Fuck if I know. And you use my share—my $660,000—to pay me a hundred grand a year until the money runs out."

I could practically see the hamster wheel spinning.

It was a big favor, and I'd asked him for a reason. No one was better at finding loopholes and telling the IRS to fuck off. It was nobody's business how much money he had, and there were likely no records of his savings. Which made him a good candidate. It wasn't illegal to pump private funds into a business.

"You wanna look good on paper with a taxed income," he stated.

I knew he'd get it.

I nodded.

"Up your credit score, be able to get loans," he continued.

That was exactly it.

"Yes."

He lit up another smoke with his old one. "I'd do that without the extra money, kid."

Did that mean...? Could I breathe out? Was he agreeing?

"What's Boone sayin' about all this?" he asked.

"Well, unlike me, he has a profession," I answered. "Any auto shop would be lucky to have him. He's on board with the idea and thinks it's smarter you hire me since he can get a job easier." The fucker just had to *try*.

The reason I'd had more gigs than Boone the past four years was because he didn't like working alone—and he lacked the confidence to be in charge. That'd always been our dynamic. I took the wheel; he fixed the car. So to speak. Then we'd split the money.

Darius lifted a shoulder in a slight shrug. "I don't see any problems. We'll get the paperwork started as soon as I get home."

Oh, fuck yeah!

A breath of relief gusted out of me, and I dragged a hand over my face.

"I'm almost insulted that you look so relieved," he chuckled. "Since when have we not helped one another out in this family, Casey?"

"I know, but—I don't know. This is different." Holy shit, I couldn't wait to tell Boone. "Thank you, Darius. Seriously."

He inclined his head. "Anytime. I just have a small condition."

"Name it."

"Buy that house for your family and make sure there's AC in the Airstream," he said. "Gray and I will need a guest room when we visit."

I grinned. "Consider it done."

EPILOGUE
348 POP-TARTS LATER

O kay, so how long was I gonna stand here and hold this?

I wiped my forehead and eyed the pool. Ace had Emma over, and the two were taking full advantage of the two big inflatable pool chairs with cupholders. They were the biggest we could find, one hot pink for me, one neon green for Boone. We would've bought a third, but then there wouldn't be any room left to swim and actually see the water.

"Girls, do you need more sunscreen?" I asked.

Ace sighed dramatically—several years too early for obnoxious preteen behavior. "We're already pasty white with the stuff."

All right, all right.

I squinted for the sun and peered up at the aluminum tent pole I was holding in place. I didn't know what else to call it. Boone was in charge of handyman shit, and he'd bought it. Several of them, actually. This was the last one.

I liked the house all right. It wasn't beige. It was terra-cotta. And stucco, of course. A bit cookie-cutter, with all the houses on our street similar, but it didn't bother me. Our house sat at the very end of the street, so in the backyard, all we saw was desert and mountains shifting in yellow, green, and red. Sunsets and sunrises around here took my fucking breath away. It was the backyard that had sealed the deal for me. The desertscape, the absolute peace, the babbling stream that ran right off our property, on the other side of the waist-high wall.

Although, I really dug the floor plan of our first real home too. It was nice to have our own bedroom. Ace loved her room too. She had the upstairs almost all to herself, except for our home office.

Letting out a breath, I wiped more sweat from my forehead and wondered what the hell was taking Boone so long.

I wasn't gonna bitch, though. He'd gone above and beyond to give me my backyard campsite.

The little Airstream was in place, and he'd built a barbecue area around it with his bare hands. A wooden framework surrounded the Airstream, creating both a step to get into the bullet as well as a narrow deck for Ace to keep her flowers and cacti. It was her new thing. She'd spent her allowance on pots, seeds, and soil all spring. And paint, because the pots had to be colorful.

She was my daughter.

"Dad, can Emma and I bake cookies?" Ace asked.

Yeah, get out of the sun. "Go for it. There's cookie dough in the fridge," I replied. "Don't touch the white chocolate macadamia, though. That's for Daddy."

"Got it!" She tumbled into the water with a Coke can I hoped was empty, and she swam over to the ladder. Emma was hot on her tail, and the two ran across the little lawn to grab their towels by the doors. Since we were building this outdoor area down here, we'd made the original deck a lot smaller. It actually reminded me of the porch we'd had before. Just enough space for a table and chairs so we could have dinner.

I didn't want a damn table near my firepit. It would ruin the whole atmosphere.

Boone finally stepped out—with his toolbox—and he could not look hotter. Jeans, no shoes, no shirt, all tatted up, a bit sweaty.

"You know how to seduce me," I said.

He smirked. "You're easy, baby." He smacked a kiss to my lips before setting the toolbox on the stone edge of the firepit.

"That's your fault, not mine." I looked down at the tent pole and where it was stuck in the ground. "I think the cement has dried." I couldn't wiggle the pole as much anymore.

He'd drilled a hole straight through the stone tile and stuck the pole down there, and then he'd taped a level to the pole and told me to hold it in place while he filled the leftover space with cement.

"It takes twenty-four hours to dry, but it should've settled a bit now."

My handyman was handy.

I didn't know what impressed me the most, the firepit he'd made with stone and mortar or...no, now I knew. The wooden staircase he'd built along the end of the Airstream. I'd thought it would just be a few steps to cover the trailer hitch, but it turned out he had plans for the roof of the Airstream. Now we could climb up there and lie down on a cushy mat just like we used to do in the bed of his truck growing up. He was giving me my favorite memories from our childhood and beyond.

"Okay, I think you can let go now." He swiped his thumb around the cement edge, smoothing the surface. "Where did you put the lights?"

"I'll get them." They were just inside the Airstream. Ace and I had picked them out online. Instead of regular bistro lights, we'd gone with a lantern design. They were tiny and colorful.

Fuck, I was excited. Boone had been at it all spring, while I had focused on installing our technology and security system inside the house. Everything was coming together now. Just a few final touches to go. Ace wanted to paint the walls in her room, and Mom thought we needed new cupboards in the kitchen.

I'd let her handle that. I didn't give a fuck.

Right this moment, I only cared about finishing our campsite. I wanted to take a photo and send it to Darius, letting him know we were ready to have him and his partner over for a visit. The silver bullet didn't have much, but there was a bed, AC, a small fridge and freezer, and a stereo. All the things we could need for a perfect evening out here.

Boone was attaching a hook to the top of the pole when I returned with the two boxes of lights.

"I don't think you realize how happy this is making me," I said.

He sent me a sideways smile and tested the durability of the hook. "I have a feeling."

Possibly because I had a way of mauling him at the end of the day.

"Didn't I fucking tell you we needed a house?" he added. "You might be the brains at work, but I know you. I've had these plans in my head for years. I know what you like."

He wasn't wrong.

"You have good ideas sometimes." I smirked.

Speaking of work, I should get ready soon. I needed a shower.

Tonight would go well—gut feeling. The guy was eager, and I was fairly certain he had a buyer lined up already. That'd been the case the last two times he'd bought something from us.

Most of AJ Lange's watch collection and the cash from his wall safe had given us our house. Tonight, I was selling the last timepiece. It was worth forty grand; we were selling it for thirty.

"Anything else you want me to do before I get ready to meet the buyer?" I asked.

Boone squinted, glancing around the barbecue area as he fastened a lantern to the tent pole. "I don't think so. I gotta bring the chairs from the garage and attach the canvas. That's about it."

That wasn't so little. The canvas ceiling would cover most of the barbecue area, except for the firepit, and half the pool. Nobody was getting skin cancer on my watch. Mom had sent me this article a while ago, about skin cancer cases rising in Nevada, and it'd freaked me the fuck out.

It was funny—and by funny, I meant fucking awful—how having everything you'd never even dared to dream of having made you terrified to lose it all.

As soon as I pulled into the driveway and killed the engine, I could hear music coming from the other side of the house. I smelled food too. Boone must've gotten started on dinner.

I grabbed my bag from the passenger's seat and left the car. Ma had given me the bag for Christmas. Worn leather, perfect fit for a small laptop. I bet she hadn't considered that it would be a perfect bag to keep money in from illegal sales, but that's what she got for having Boone and me as her kids.

Before I joined my family for dinner, I snuck upstairs and into our office.

Opening our safe was essentially foreplay. I was good to go for a hard fuck after every visit in here.

I emptied the laptop bag of money and stacked it with the rest.

It felt good, I couldn't lie. We'd laid low for months, focusing on creating our home, Boone finding a job, and me researching our future options. After the summer, we were gonna take on the home of a rich, retired hedge fund dude. He had a collection of cars we wanted to get our hands on, something I wouldn't have considered if it weren't for a recent connection I'd made. Boone and I only had to steal them. A guy from Philadelphia would pay up front before selling them overseas.

It was gonna be fun.

After a quick trip to the bathroom and changing into more comfortable clothes, I trailed downstairs again and out onto the patio, where I came to a stop and just gawked at my dream come true.

Jesus Christ. A big smile took over my face as Boone glanced my way, and I couldn't fucking believe him. He grinned back and tipped a beer bottle at me.

This was home. Fuck me twice and call me Santa, I was gonna grow old in this house, and no one could stop me.

"Hi, Daddy! The hot dogs are almost done!" Ace announced.

I crossed the lawn and took in my surroundings. The canvas stretching over the pool and barbecue area, the lanterns, the chairs—he'd painted them! There were four Adirondack chairs around the firepit, and he'd painted them in different colors. He'd only told me he was gonna "treat" them with something. Then the blankets Mom and Ace had bought, one for each chair.

Not a single goddamn thing was beige.

"You're amazing," I told Boone. "In-fucking-credible." I walked up to him and kissed him.

He smiled into the kiss. "How did it go?"

"As planned." We could talk more later. I touched his cheek briefly, then returned my attention to the campsite. And the food. I was starving. "We're gonna spend a lot of evenings here, aren't we?"

"Fuck yeah." Ace left her seat to poke at the hot dogs on the grill. "I think they're done."

As if on cue, my stomach snarled. We took our seats and passed the ketchup, mustard, buns, and relish between us, and I had nothing to say. I just reveled and let Boone and Ace do the talking. Ace had been invited for a movie night at Emma's house soon, and Boone asked the right questions about parental supervision and whatnot.

The next topic was the summer camp Ace would be attending in a couple weeks. She spoke animatedly about the excursions they'd be taking, and by the third activity, Boone had to remind her to breathe.

"I'm just excited!" she exclaimed. "I've never gone on a Jet Ski before."

I grinned around a mouthful of food at a memory that surfaced and reached for my beer.

"It's fun until your kid brother takes a sharp turn and throws you off it," Boone replied wryly.

I coughed around a laugh.

Ace giggled and widened her eyes at me. "Did you do that?"

"I would never," I bullshitted.

Boone snorted and shook his head in amusement.

At midnight, the neighborhood was dead silent.

Boone and I killed all the lights and climbed up on the roof of the Airstream.

It seemed he'd done work up here too. The foam mat was reinforced along the sides, making it level so we wouldn't fall off the damn thing.

I knew our area had a spectacular view of Vegas; all I had to do was turn around. But I wasn't here to see the city glittering in the night. I was here to disappear into a bubble with just Boone, and it seemed he was extra eager for the same tonight. We got comfortable on our backs and let out a big breath in unison.

"Everything okay?" I asked quietly.

"More than." He threaded our fingers together. "Just been a long day. It feels good to have everything done."

I squeezed his hand.

As my eyes adjusted to the dark, more and more stars appeared in the sky.

Until there were millions of them.

Slow, deep breaths.

The day faded away bit by bit.

How many times over the years had Boone and I found ourselves in complete silence in the middle of the desert, just staring up at the night sky? It'd become transcendent for me. Because right here, right now, I could visit myself at any age and see us in the exact same position. At eleven, when we went camping with a friend's family. At fourteen, after flunking a test. At sixteen, after being suspended from school for fighting.

We'd driven straight out into the nothingness after we'd learned about Tia's death too. We'd been so fucking scared.

We didn't need to escape from screw-ups anymore, though. At some point, it'd turned into a break that just reenergized us. At the same time as it centered us, calmed us down, brought us peace.

I lifted our clasped hands and kissed his fingertips.

He sighed contentedly. "I love you."

"I love you too."

I flicked my gaze from one celestial body to the next and folded my free hand under my head.

It could be overwhelming up here. On the one hand, I'd never felt stronger. My future had never looked this bright. I had my family. Ace. She owned my sorry ass. Boone, my brother, my partner in crime, the father of my daughter, the love of my fucking life. Mom. Her patience... Friends. My health. A home. Then on the other hand, underneath the stars and surrounded by my desert, I was tiny and insignificant. I was nothing in the grand scheme of things. No one would tell stories about me in a thousand years. I wasn't gonna end up in history books or leave a mark on this earth.

So I had the present. I had right now.

I had the rest of my life to show Boone and Ace that at least my devotion to them was eternal.

Boone gave my hand a warm squeeze. "Are you thinking existential things?"

"Like you wouldn't believe." I tilted my head and looked at him. "Are you thinking about what's for dinner tomorrow?"

He rumbled a drowsy chuckle and turned on his side. "No... I'm just...blissed out."

Good word for how I felt too. "Same here."

He inched closer and kissed me softly, and it didn't go unnoticed how he slipped a hand down my sweats. "Do you think the Airstream can handle a fucking?"

I grinned lazily and shifted against his touch. "I think it's our responsibility to find out."

He hummed. "It's possible I brought lube."

I exhaled a chuckle, and damn, he was getting me hard too

fast. Too easily. "I'd be disappointed if you hadn't. How do you want me?"

"Behind me. Buried deep until you fill my ass with your come."

Yeah, okay, we were done stargazing.

Pssst. Keep reading.

A QUICK QUESTION

Do you want more of Case and Boone?

As Darius Quinn's cousins, Casey and Boone are part of a much bigger operation, and if you're curious about Darius's mission and seeing the O'Sullivan boys again, the *Auctioned Series* might be for you. *The Job* takes place between the third and fourth books in the *Auctioned Series*, and Casey and Boone will make appearances in both *Played* and *Finished*.

The Auctioned Series is a five-book journey packed with action, nail-biting suspense, family, and love.

#1 Auctioned | #2 Stranded | #3 Deserted | #4 Played | #5 Finished

Gray Nolan is just another happy-go-lucky college dude when his ordinary existence gets interrupted and he becomes a human trafficking statistic. Darius Quinn is a restaurant owner who has vowed never again to find himself in a situation like this. His days as a private military contractor are over. No more missions, no more risks, no more personal attachments. Yet, here he is, searching for a small town's favorite son.

Their story begins with a brutal auction out at sea, when Darius steps out of the shadows and comes face-to-face with the broken young man he's just bought.

In Gray and Darius's fight for freedom and a future where they aren't haunted by the ghosts of their pasts, they'll make you laugh, cry, swoon just a bit, and possibly yell at your e-reader.

MORE FROM CARA

Cara freely admits she's addicted to revisiting the men and women who yammer in her head, and several of her characters cross over in other titles. If you enjoyed this book, you might like the following.

Auctioned
MM | Suspense Romance | Hurt/Comfort | Trauma

At twenty-one, Gray Nolan became a human trafficking statistic. He and seven other young men were taken aboard a luxurious yacht where they would be auctioned off to the highest bidder. Tortured, shattered, and almost defeated, he watched his new owner step out of the shadows in a swirl of his own cigarette smoke.

Breathless
MMM | The Game Series, #3 | BDSM | S/M | Daddykink | Standalone

"Will you beat me without knowing why I want it?"
    I'm used to rejection by Sadists at this point. No one wants to beat me or skip aftercare; they wanna talk and get all up in my business—where they don't freaking belong. But I give it one more try when I spot River and Reese Tenley at a kink party. The only thing bigger than them is their reputation as hardcore Sadists and former military. To the memories of grief and why I'm seeking punishment, I ask them to hurt me.
    "Sure. It's your funeral."

Aftermath
MM | Kidnapping Drama | Suspense Romance | Hurt/Comfort | Standalone

Austin Huntley and Cameron Nash are like night and day. One is a wholesome family man and works in a nice office. The other is an antisocial car mechanic on the spectrum with a short fuse. But after being kidnapped and spending five months together in a small cell, life will never be the same, and they can't go a day without seeing each other. This is their aftermath.

This Life I
MF | Mafia Romance | Arranged Marriage | Comedy | Loyalty

Finnegan O'Shea's plan was to get rid of the Sons of Munsters' gobshite boss, the man who'd murdered Finn's grandfather. A family man had more to lose and was generally less likely to take any risks, so that was who Finn would become. A family man. A top earner. He'd get close to the inner circle and... Okay, now wasn't the time to get ahead of himself. First he had to find a damn wife. Someone sweet and compliant who wouldn't get in the way. Emilia Porter seemed perfect—until her claws came out and Finn realized he'd met his match.

Check out Cara's entire collection at www.caradeewrites.com, and don't forget to sign up for her newsletter so you don't miss any new releases, updates on book signings, free outtakes, giveaways, and much more.

ABOUT CARA

I'm often awkwardly silent or, if the topic interests me, a chronic rambler. In other words, I can discuss writing forever and ever. Fiction, in particular. The love story—while a huge draw and constantly present—is secondary for me, because there's so much more to writing romance fiction than just making two (or more) people fall in love and have hot sex.

There's a world to build, characters to develop, interests to create, and a topic or two to research thoroughly.

Every book is a challenge for me, an opportunity to learn something new, and a puzzle to piece together. I want my characters to come to life, and the only way I know to do that is to give them substance—passions, history, goals, quirks, and strong opinions—and to let them evolve.

I want my men and women to be relatable. That means allowing room for everyday problems and, for lack of a better word, flaws. My characters will never be perfect.

Wait...this was supposed to be about me, not my writing.

I'm a writey person who loves to write. Always wanderlusting, twitterpating, kinking, cooking, baking, and geeking. There's time for hockey and family, too. But mostly, I just love to write.

~Cara.

Get social with Cara
www.caradeewrites.com
www.camassiacove.com
Facebook: @caradeewrites
Twitter: @caradeewrites
Instagram: @caradeewrites